He appeared out of nowhere like a knight in shining armor.

"Oh...." Leah's eyes widened.

Kelly followed her friend's glassy-eyed stare as a shiny black sports car pulled up into the parking space. Kelly forgot to breathe. The car was sleek and dangerous-looking, but that was nothing compared to the man dressed in black who stepped out the door that slid up and forward like the raised wing of some evil dark bird.

Reece Maddox strolled toward her, all supple, masculine grace, as if it was the most natural thing in the world for him to do. Kelly put her hand to her temple. She did not want this sudden rush of unwanted anticipation zinging through her. She exhaled sharply.

"What are you *doing* here? How did you even know where *here* is?"

Reece removed the band of dark sunglasses that covered his eyes. "We have a problem."

DANI SINCLAIR

MIDNIGHT PRINCE

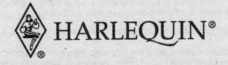

HARLEQUIN®

TORONTO • NEW YORK • LONDON
AMSTERDAM • PARIS • SYDNEY • HAMBURG
STOCKHOLM • ATHENS • TOKYO • MILAN • MADRID
PRAGUE • WARSAW • BUDAPEST • AUCKLAND

In memory of Ms. Possum.
And for Roger, Chip, Dan and Barb as always.

ISBN-13: 978-0-373-88777-4
ISBN-10:   0-373-88777-9

MIDNIGHT PRINCE

ABOUT THE AUTHOR

An avid reader, Dani Sinclair didn't discover romance novels until her mother loaned her one when she'd come for a visit. Dani's been hooked on the genre ever since. But she didn't take up writing seriously until her two sons were grown. *Mystery Baby* premiered for Harlequin Intrigue in 1996, and Dani's kept her computer busy ever since. Her third novel, *Better Watch Out,* was a RITA® Award finalist in 1998. Dani lives outside Washington, D.C., a place she's found to be a great source for both intrigue and humor!

You can write to her in care of the Harlequin Reader Service.

Books by Dani Sinclair

HARLEQUIN INTRIGUE
658—SCARLET VOWS
730—THE FIRSTBORN*
736—THE SECOND SISTER*
742—THE THIRD TWIN*
827—SECRET CINDERELLA
854—D.B. HAYES, DETECTIVE
870—RETURN TO STONY RIDGE*
935—BEAUTIFUL BEAST
970—SLEEPING BEAUTY SUSPECT
1003—MIDNIGHT PRINCE

*Heartskeep

CAST OF CHARACTERS

Reece Maddox—The international jet-setter has more than one secret that may just cost him his life. But he'll save Kelly's if it's the last thing he does.

Kelly O'Donnell—She'll find out what really happened to her father, even if it means exposing the mysterious business partner her father trusted.

Eugene O'Donnell—His sudden death is a mystery. His legacy to his daughter is Custom Concepts, the construction company he built with James Prince.

James Prince—The secretive millionaire isn't just reclusive. Kelly's mysterious new partner has never been seen by *anyone* who works at Custom Concepts.

Heath Brockmorton—The British playboy has been Reece's friend for years—hasn't he?

Rebecca Holliman—Heath's lady friend is a working woman whom Kelly likes from the start.

Oliver Kendall—Part of the jet set crowd—is he as harmless as he seems?

Curtis Long—Reece has known the wealthy businessman for years. It seems only logical to seek his help when things go wrong.

Mark Ramsey—The security specialist works for Reece, Kelly and the elusive James Prince, but where do his loyalties really lie?

Mr. Smith—The government agent has a job to do. Nothing and no one else matters.

Leah Wickliff—Kelly's friend calls her new partner the Midnight Prince, because he only comes out after dark…

Chapter One

The computer's soft glow provided the only light in the dark room. Too much light as far as Reece Maddox was concerned. Any moment now a security guard might see light where there shouldn't be any and send someone to check it out. The party was spread across several rooms, all on the far side of the building. He needed to get back to the boisterous affair before someone other than his date noted his absence.

The last file finished loading. He pulled the flash drive from the computer, aware that he had taken far too long to find and move the files he'd been sent to find. The sound of male laughter from beyond the closed door carried to where he crouched beside the desk. Several men, talking freely, were heading in his direction. He doubted his host would believe he'd been looking for a bathroom if he was found in here.

Reece stood. There was no time to shut the computer down. He shoved the flash drive in his pocket and surveyed the room. The bank of second-story windows was the only other way out. Not an optimum choice. Still… He ran to the window and peered down. He'd break his fool neck.

Or he could let the men nearly at the door do it for him.

Reece opened the window. Too late, he spied the sensor. To his partial relief, no audible alarm sounded, but he knew he'd just tripped a silent one somewhere. Swearing softly, he eyed the rough stone facing on the side of the house. His expensive Italian leather shoes weren't made for rock climbing. Too bad there wasn't any choice unless he could reach the balcony that jutted out a short distance away. He could hang from that and drop and he'd probably only break his leg.

If he'd ever needed luck, it was now. He climbed onto the windowsill and leaped for the wrought iron railing.

Lady Luck smiled. His right hand caught the bottom rail, nearly wrenching his arm from its socket as he dangled above the ground.

Biting his lip against the pain, his feet sought and found a niche in the stone facade while his left hand did the same. That took some of the strain from his right arm and shoulder as light suddenly bloomed in the room he'd just left.

No time for finesse. Reece let go of the rail and tried to relax his muscles as he dropped. The stretch of manicured bushes running along the base of the wall broke his fall, but it was hardly pain or noise free. Excited voices were suddenly raised above him.

Reece scrambled to his feet and pasted himself against the rough stone. His dark hair and black tuxedo should help him melt into the shadows as he inched his way toward the brightly lit front of the estate. Security would come from the rear of the grounds, but it wouldn't take them long to alert the entire staff to watch for a prowler.

Barely out of sight of the floodlights, he paused at the corner to brush dirt and greenery from his clothes and strip off the latex gloves. He shoved them into a pocket and finger combed his hair. There was no time to do more. He walked toward the well-lit front door as if he had every right to be out for a stroll amid the landscaping.

Lady Luck was still in a generous mood. A large group of noisy partygoers was coming out the front door, talking and laughing as they moved past the bored security guards. One of those people was Curtis Long. Luck couldn't have provided anyone better for his needs. The portly importer looked weary while his wife chatted animatedly with a young couple who were probably friends of their son.

Reece calculated his odds and stepped over the raised stone wall that edged the front steps as one of the women in the group dropped her bag while searching for her vehicle's claim ticket.

Reece bent with the other males present to help collect lipstick, coins and assorted items that had tumbled out. The woman giggled tipsily and apologized in fluent Italian.

Thanking the luck, he maneuvered himself alongside the older man. "Evening, Curtis."

"Reece," Curtis greeted in surprise. "Didn't see you there."

"I wanted to say hello earlier, but never got the chance. You're looking well." In fact, Reece thought he looked rather drawn and pasty. His breathing was audible as he handed the woman several coins.

"Doctor says I need to lose weight and cut my stress," he griped. "You try running my business and doing either one. What does he expect? Damn fool."

Reece pasted on a sympathetic smile. "Doctors." It seemed a noncommittal enough reply. "Are you and your wife going to the embassy party in Milan tomorrow?"

"No, thank God. We've got an early flight back to the States first thing in the morning. She insists I see some specialist in Alexandria."

"Wives are like that."

"How would you know? According to my son you're still running free."

"So far," Reece agreed. "And so is he unless,

something has changed since I saw him in San Moritz. Are you flying into Dulles, then?"

Curtis nodded. They both took a step down as a second throng of people crowded onto the small portico and more youths were disbursed to locate parked cars and limousines.

"I hate these transcontinental flights, but my wife loves Italy."

A third security man had joined the guards and spoke in hushed but apparently urgent tones. Reece weighed his options while trying to appear as though he wasn't paying any attention. "And how is your son doing since I saw him last?"

"That boy of mine needs to learn a few hard truths. He still wants to be a damn carpenter."

Reece breathed a silent sigh of relief. "He always did like to work with his hands."

"Fine, make it a hobby. But a carpenter, for God's sake! You don't make any money as a carpenter. He wants to build houses."

"I know a man who does that."

Curtis eyed him sharply. "He make any money at it?"

"Enough to get by."

The snort drew his wife's gaze in their direction and Reece nodded a greeting at her.

"That's what I've been trying to tell him," Curtis griped. "It won't pay. He needs to come into business with me and play carpenter in his spare time."

"Maybe you should have him talk with my friend. Gene might change his mind."

"Think so?"

Reece shrugged as if it didn't matter. "Gene will tell him the truth, at any rate."

"That's not a bad idea."

Reece reached for one of his cards and a pen and printed Gene's name and number on the back. "The irony is, I was scheduled to fly home tomorrow night and bring Gene some files from an Italian builder he knows over here. I met with the man right before coming to this party and now it looks like there's a good chance I'm going to miss my flight. My date informs me she has her heart set on attending that embassy thing."

"Be careful, Reece. Sooner or later, one of these ladies is going to put a ring on your finger as well as through your nose."

"Not a chance," he assured the older man. "But it generally pays to please a lady. Is there any chance I could prevail on you to take this flash drive back for me? I hate not delivering on a promise. I could call and ask Gene to meet you tomorrow after you go through customs. You could arrange for him to talk to Steve at the same time."

"No problem. I'd like to meet your friend."

"Thanks." Neither guard was looking in their direction as Reece handed him the flash drive. Their attention was on the first of the cars that had pulled up at the bottom of the stairs. Immediately behind came a sleek, black limousine.

"That's my ride, I'm afraid." Curtis nodded toward the limousine. "We're taking Delta 698. Tell your friend I look forward to chatting with him." He pocketed the drive.

"Great. Thanks again. I owe you one."

"Not if your friend helps me talk some sense into that boy of mine."

They shook hands and Reece headed for the front door while Curtis separated his wife from the other couple. The security guards, looking far more alert now than they had a few minutes earlier, stopped him when Reece would have walked back inside.

"It's okay," Reece assured them in Italian. "I was just walking a friend outside to say goodbye."

"Your name, *signore?*"

Not good, but no help for it. "Reece Maddox."

The speaker looked him over coldly while his companion checked the name against a roster on his clipboard. Reece hoped Lady Luck hadn't strayed yet. Any sign of a tear or stain on his clothes at this point would put him in more trouble than he was apt to survive. His shoulder and back were aching abominably now that some of the adrenaline had worn off.

"I'll need to see your invitation, sir."

"No problem." Reece fished the card from his jacket pocket and waited while the man looked it over and the second man nodded confirmation of his name.

They waved him inside. Reece strode purposefully back toward the ballroom while hoping he hadn't missed a camera in the upstairs office. Fighting instincts that urged him to turn around and make a run for it, he strolled forward with every appearance of calm and spotted his friend, Heath Brockmorton, leading an obviously inebriated Oliver Kendall toward the front door.

"Need some help?"

"Actually, I wouldn't say no. Oliver here needs to find his driver."

"Party's not over," Oliver protested blearily.

"It is for you, chum."

Reece helped Heath guide Oliver back the way he'd come. Oliver's good looks and likeable demeanor gave him entrée to the fringes of a world he craved despite the fact his family fortunes weren't what he wanted them to be.

"Got a lady waitin' for me," Oliver protested.

Reece raised questioning eyebrows at Heath. His friend shook his head. "The lady's married."

"Thash okay."

"No, it really isn't. Her husband is a fencing

master and terribly jealous. You really don't want to get involved with her."

"Tired," Oliver complained.

"Yes, and you'll feel much worse come morning," Heath assured him unkindly. "He's taking an early morning flight home."

Reece winced. Probably the same flight as Curtis and his wife. However, Oliver would be lucky to make it out of bed by noon. "Cab?"

"Definitely. I don't know which woman he came with but she's better off on her own."

The guard with the clipboard took one look at the trio and sent a youth scurrying for one of the cabs they had on call. Reece and Heath saw Oliver off and the guards passed them back inside with a wave.

"Don't know about you, chum, but I've had enough frivolity for one evening. Thanks for the help."

Reece nodded and they parted. He made it a point to stop and talk with several more people on his way through the crowd, aware of a subtle undercurrent of tension to the party now. His date was chatting with a small group, mostly men, and her annoyed expression saved him from suggesting they leave. She announced as much with narrowed eyes and the sort of pleated brow that would, in later years, form wrinkles. It proved ridiculously easy to leave her at the door of her hotel suite a short time later, her sharp complaints echoing in his head.

Reece really hadn't expected to make it off the estate. That he had didn't mean he was out of danger. Instead of heading for his own room, he sought out the hotel bar downstairs and the bank of pay phones near the restrooms. The connection overseas proved clear and Gene answered on the third ring, sounding preoccupied.

"It's me," Reece announced without using names. "I need one of those favors we talked about."

He pictured the sandy haired man sitting up straighter. "Shoot."

One of the many things Reece liked about Eugene O'Donnell was his friend's easy acceptance of any given situation. There were few people he trusted the way he trusted Gene. Reece gave him the information on Curtis Long's arrival. Unfortunately, there was no way he could avoid using that name.

"Do me a favor and meet his plane when he lands. His son wants to be a builder, but Curtis would rather he'd join the family business."

"That right?"

Gene's voice was alert, listening for nuances.

"I told him you'd be honest about the ups and downs. And since there's a chance I might be delayed getting back tomorrow I asked him to pass along those files from your Italian friend."

Since Gene didn't have an Italian friend to

Reece's knowledge, he was relieved when the older man went along without question.

"Great."

"But I still haven't found you a replacement for that jacket I ruined."

Reece hadn't ruined anything of Gene's so his silence was understandable.

"Did you ever try that dry cleaner I recommended?"

"No." Comprehension filled his tone. "I'll give him a call tomorrow. Don't worry about it."

"Have them try getting the stain out and be sure and tell them to charge it to me. They'll even come pick it up for you."

"Okay. I'll do that. You going to be delayed long?"

The concern in his tone warmed Reece. "I hope not. A friend of mine wants to attend some embassy shindig in Milan tomorrow. I'm hoping to talk her out of it. Personally, I'm ready for a hot dog and a beer."

Gene was ex-military, ex-special forces. He'd never asked what agency Reece worked for, but, given the way the two of them had met when Gene came to his rescue in an alley several years ago, Gene had more than an inkling about the sort of work he did. Reece had once told him who to call in an emergency and what words to use. Confident his friend would understand what he wanted him to do with the drive, Reece relaxed.

"I've got beer chilling right now," Gene offered. "I'll put a hot dog on the grill as soon as you get back."

"Knew I could count on you. I'll call you."

"Do that. And take care or yourself."

"Of course."

Hanging up, Reece rubbed at his shoulder, hoping a shower and some ice would minimize the pain. He was too old to be jumping out of second-story windows and he wasn't totally convinced he'd pulled this escape off yet.

He started to dial a familiar number to report in when he saw two policemen rapidly approaching. Yeah. He'd known escape wasn't going to be that easy.

NINE DAYS LATER Reece slipped into the deep shadow of a wide cedar tree and stared down into the brightly lit garden apartment at the bottom of the slope. No drapes covered the sliding-glass door, so he watched as Kelly O'Donnell laid her head on her arms on top of the pile of scattered papers on the table in front of her. The defeat in every slim line of her body tore at his heart.

He shared every bit of her grief even though the two of them had never met. He knew her, every freckle, every smile. She was a lovely, vibrant, utterly feminine version of her father.

The pain that rose inside over that loss left him

gritting his teeth. He forced it down while wondering if there really was release to be found in tears. He would have liked to shed a few for what had happened, but there were no do-overs in this life, only regrets.

Clipping the small device to the cell phone to distort his voice, Reece pressed the speed-dial button and watched as her head jerked up a few seconds later. The spill of red-gold hair tumbled like a curtain about her face. She brushed it aside to wipe quickly at eyes and cheeks before reaching for the phone beside her.

"Hello?"

Her voice was softer than he expected and coated by a husky layer of suppressed tears. "Is this Kelly O'Donnell?"

He watched her glance at the clock, saw her body stiffen in wariness. "I'm sorry to call so late," he added hastily. "But I just got back into town and learned what happened. You don't know me, but my name is…James Prince."

Her fingers tightened on the receiver. A flicker of hope mixed with determination replaced the despair on her expressive face. "I know *of* you, Mr. Prince. You're…you were my father's business partner."

"Yes. I just learned of his unfortunate accident."

"My father didn't have an accident, Mr. Prince. He was murdered."

His body tensed. She was right, but there was no way she could have known that for certain. "The police said—"

"The police are incompetent."

Shoving back the chair she stood and began to pace the area. A small, slender woman, she was unconsciously graceful. Years of gymnastics and martial arts training had given her a sleek, well-toned body.

"My father might possibly have gotten into a brawl with someone at the trailer that night, but he wasn't drunk because he doesn't drink. Not anymore."

"His blood alcohol level was 0.3 and there was a mostly empty bottle of scotch at the scene with two glasses and—"

She stopped his recitation. "I've spoken with the police, Mr. Prince. At length. I really don't care what they say."

Amazing how much scorn she could infuse into a simple sentence.

"That scotch is one of the reasons I *know* he was murdered," she continued. "He kept that unopened bottle in his filing cabinet for years. I'm not sure exactly why because, even when he used to drink, my father never touched scotch. He literally couldn't stomach the smell of it. No, Mr. Prince, someone forced that scotch down his throat and killed him and probably that other man, as well, no matter what the local police believe."

There was certainty in her voice, not a shred of doubt. She stopped pacing and crossed to the patio window to stare out at the chilly dark night. Automatically, he drew back. There was no way she could see him, but he stopped moving and held very still, nevertheless, because she seemed to be looking right at him.

"*One* of the reasons?"

Turning away, she resumed her pacing. He watched her firm breasts rise and fall beneath the pale white sweater.

"The police claim the other man's lit cigarette started the fire, but Dad didn't allow smoking in the trailer. Not ever."

"Perhaps that's what they were fighting about."

She ignored the interruption as if he hadn't spoken. "He also didn't store flammables inside the trailer. Someone took them from the job site and put them inside so the room would fill with fumes. That fire was not an accident."

She was absolutely right on all counts.

"Believe what you like, Mr. Prince. The police do. I expect you want a status report on the business."

Her flat tone didn't quite mask the edge of despondency. She moved back to the table, lifted several papers and launched into a scenario he would have anticipated if he hadn't been jet-lagged and seriously sleep deprived.

"The trailer was totally destroyed, of course. You can expect the insurance company to drag their feet over liability. The lumber and masonry companies have put a stop to our scheduled deliveries until all moneys due are paid in full. Future orders are to be paid up front. I paid the crew through next week, but there isn't much for them to do if the supplies don't start arriving again. The company accounts are frozen, of course, but I'm not sure there was enough in there to cover all the bills we owe, anyhow. Death brings the bill collectors scuttling from under their rocks in a big hurry. I don't know, for sure, exactly who or how much we owe because the invoices were in the trailer and they're mostly wet ashes at this point. Since I had no way to get in touch with you—"

"I'll transfer enough money into a new business account to cover the outstanding debts. And, don't worry, I'll take care of the suppliers, as well. You don't need to feel responsible for the company, any longer."

She dropped the papers and went rigid. Her voice chilled. "I beg to differ, Mr. Prince. Were you or were you not my father's silent partner?"

"I was, yes. As I said, I'll take care of things and repay all of your out-of-pocket expenses."

"That will be greatly appreciated, but you're

missing the point here. You and my father were partners. As my father's only heir, I inherit his share of Custom Concepts. That makes *us* partners now."

His mouth opened, but for several seconds he couldn't think of a thing to say. She stood ramrod straight, five feet two inches of feminine determination.

"Are you saying you intend to continue running the business?"

"Absolutely. My father put his heart into this company and it appears I suddenly need a job. Coincidentally, here is one for the taking."

She was serious. "You're serious."

"Of course I am."

"Kel— Ms. O'Donnell, what do you know about running a construction company?"

"I'm a business major, Mr. Prince. I have an MBA, as a matter of fact. Running a business is what I've been training to do for the past several years."

He knew she had received her advance degree two weeks ago. He'd been there, sitting through the graduation ceremony with her father, though she didn't know that. He might have met her then if he hadn't been called away abruptly before Gene could find her in the crowd.

"That may be so, but not a construction company," he protested. "I think your father had other hopes for you."

"My father is dead, Mr. Prince. He had many hopes. So did I. If you're worried about your investment, don't be. I grew up on construction sites all over the United States. What I don't know, I'll learn. My dad has a terrific foreman, a good crew and I know an architect if the one he was using won't work with me. Most of our crew has been with us since Dad started this business. I can handle the company."

"I believe you." Surprisingly, he did. "I can see you've given this some thought," and it was totally unexpected. Reece had planned to sell off what he could and buy her out to keep her as safe and as far from trouble as possible. It was the least he owed her father.

"Construction is still mostly considered a male-driven industry," he pointed out.

"Are you a chauvinist, Mr. Prince?"

The challenge made his lips curve. "Not really, but there are those in this particular field who undoubtedly are."

"I can handle them."

He wouldn't bet against her. "No doubt, but I suspect things would go easier if some of your suppliers knew you had a partner, true?"

"You mean, a male partner."

"Yes."

"What are you proposing, Mr. Prince?"

"Nothing to ruffle your feathers. Merely the same

deal I had with your father. You need operating capital. I can provide that. You work for me until you're established and can afford to buy me out."

She hesitated. "That's the same deal you had with my father?"

"Basically, yes."

"So what do you get out of this?"

"Sixty percent of the profits and your goodwill."

"Fifty and I'll toss in the goodwill."

He found he could smile, after all. She was definitely Eugene's daughter. "I have the most to lose, Ms. O'Donnell."

"And I have the skills you need to run this business."

"That remains to be seen."

"Give me a chance. I'll show you what I can do."

He didn't like it. The risk was too high. The other side wasn't entirely certain Reece had been the intruder; if they had been, Reece would never have left Italy alive. The party's host ran the local government in his small seaside town so the arrival of the local *polizia* that night had come as no surprise. They had held Reece for questioning on a trumped-up charge long enough to search him and his hotel room for anything incriminating.

He wasn't sure how Heath had heard about the situation, but his friend had brought some pressure to bear and they'd finally released him. Reece had returned to his room only to discover his passport missing. Knowing he was being watched closely, he'd jumped through all the expected hoops, displayed all the normal reactions and carefully did nothing out of line. He hadn't learned Gene was dead until he finally made it back to the States. By then, the funeral was over.

Reece's agency knew for certain that Curtis Long had met with Gene and delivered the flash drive. The airport security tapes had also shown a familiar face watching the exchange. Arthur Weems had been on their watch list a long time. No doubt, Curtis Long had been tagged as the carrier because of his early morning flight home. Arthur had been sent to watch for his arrival. But he wouldn't have been there alone. At the very least, he would have had a driver waiting outside. Reece took what bitter satisfaction he could from the knowledge that Gene had managed to kill Arthur before he died himself. Unfortunately, the flash drive was gone so it had all been for nothing and a good man was dead.

Was there danger in letting Kelly continue to operate Custom Concepts? This was something she obviously wanted, a piece of her father to carry forward. Reece owed her that and more, but he couldn't risk putting her in harm's way. The agency agreed that his cover was compromised. Fortunately, his James Prince persona and his connection to Custom Concepts and the other businesses he partnered was well buried. If he kept a low profile it should be safe enough.

"Fifty-two percent, final offer." He gave her no room to wiggle.

"That makes it your company."

"Yes."

"What happens if I get the money to buy you out and you refuse to sell?"

He watched her through the glass, all rigid determination as she stared at the bare walls of the sparsely furnished apartment. Until today, the apartment had bustled with out-of-town relatives and friends. A cousin and his wife were still staying with her, but they'd gone out for the evening; Reece had taken advantage of the opportunity to call her.

"There's a risk in everything we do, Ms. O'Donnell."

Scowling, she started to prowl again. "Is this the same deal you gave my dad?"

He'd known she was intelligent. Her father was always ready to brag about her accomplishments.

"You aren't your father, Ms. O'Donnell."

"Are we talking a *Remington Steele* scenario here, Mr. Prince, with you as a figurehead? Or are you planning to take an active role?"

"My name will head up Custom Concepts. Everything will go through me, but you'll be the person running the day-to-day operations."

"You mean, I'll be a glorified employee."

"Who collects forty-eight percent of the profits," he reminded her.

"And does all the work."

His lips quirked at her wry tone. "We both know life isn't fair, Ms. O'Donnell, or I'd still be talking with your father. Take it or leave it."

Bringing up her father like that was a low blow, but it was all the warning he could give her. Continuing to keep Custom Concepts running was dangerous. It was also the best chance he had to find a link back to a subversive cell they suspected was operating in the D.C. area. Still, Reece wasn't sure if he wanted her to accept or decline the offer.

"I don't like it, but you leave me little choice," she agreed reluctantly. "You have a deal, Mr. Prince. Where do I meet you to sign the paperwork?"

"You don't." Not ever. That was one risk he wasn't willing to take. "Why don't you sleep on my offer? Think it over for a few days. I'm still willing to buy you out."

"No."

There was no wiggle room in her voice, either.

"I want our arrangement in writing, Mr. Prince."

Gene would be proud of her. "I'll have a contract drawn up and ready for you to sign in two days. The operating money will be in the business account first thing tomorrow. You'll need to go to your father's bank in the afternoon to sign the papers that will give you access."

He heard relief as she exhaled, saw it in her change of posture. He hoped he wasn't making another huge mistake.

"Your father and I had another arrangement, Ms. O'Donnell. I wish to make a similar arrangement with you. I have other interests, so papers requiring my attention will be left in the office on my desk each night. I will give you a—"

"What office? In case you missed that part, the trailer exploded and burned to the ground along with my father."

"We will be renting space in a warehouse on Granby St. I'll get the address and key to you in a day or so. The warehouse has office space as well as storage space for deliveries that don't go straight to a given job site. It's something your father and I discussed implementing several weeks ago."

"He never mentioned anything."

He wouldn't have because setting up a permanent office was something Gene hadn't wanted to do. He hadn't seen the need for the extra expense, but she couldn't know that. Frankly, Reece was surprised Kelly even knew Gene had had a partner. Gene knew how to keep his silence. That Reece was still alive was proof enough of that.

"Do you have a problem with the location?" he asked.

"Of course not."

"Then you'll be hearing from me."

"Wait! How can I reach you if something comes up?"

"You can't. Not at the moment. I'll let you know when I have a new number."

"Something wrong with this one? Your call came up marked private."

"That's how I do business, Ms. O'Donnell. I'm a very private person. Do you have a problem with that?"

"Yes, but I doubt you care."

"Not really, no." He hesitated, oddly reluctant to end this conversation. She couldn't know how much he shared her grief. In some ways, they had both just lost a father.

"Kelly, your dad was a special man. I was lucky enough to count him a friend." He missed him more than she would ever know. "He'd be very proud of the way you've held things together since his death. Try to stop worrying now and get some sleep. You're going to be very busy in the coming weeks."

And he would have to scramble hard and fast to stay ahead of her. The challenge should prove interesting.

Chapter Two

"I don't believe it. The Midnight Prince left you
flowers again?"

Kelly O'Donnell looked from the small bouquet
of irises to her new friend, Leah Wickliff, and
back again.

"Will you stop calling him that? They're a thank
you. I settled the dispute we were having with one
of the subcontractors."

"Uh-huh."

"Stop it. The flowers were a nice gesture."

"Nice. Right. I've been working for Ferinelli and
Company for two years. I've never gotten a single
dandelion, let alone a vase of irises and a box of expensive chocolates. But then, I don't work for an invisible man so I guess that makes all the difference."

"He's not invisible. He's just…"

"A vampire?"

"Stop it."

"You've only spoken to the man over the phone.

You've never seen him. *No one's* ever seen him. And the few times you've spoken with him have been late at night. He sneaks in after everyone is gone for the day to leave you messages and sign whatever needs signing and *not one person working here* has ever laid eyes on the man. Sounds like a vampire to me."

While all completely true, it sounded so much worse when Leah stated the facts out loud like that.

"You need to stop reading so many weird books. Besides, whoever heard of a vampire that wears aftershave?" Kelly loved the light spicy scent she'd come to associate with his sterile little office.

Leah brushed back her dark brown hair and grinned. "He's courting you."

"He is not!"

"Candy, flowers, love notes—sounds like courting to me."

Kelly picked up the recent note from her desk and read it out loud. *"Good work, Kelly. Have Fred hire another bricklayer for the Oakley job and, you're right, we're going to need an extra shipment of two-by-fours for next week. Tell your friend Riley to go ahead and start work on the Trefolie project. JP."* She looked pointedly at her friend. "Needs work on his poetic expressions, don't you think?"

"Okay, maybe not love notes, but come on,

what boss sends flowers and candy to his secretary all the time?"

"Partner, or administrative assistant, at the very least, if you don't mind. He's never even met me. Besides he's an old man."

"How would you know?"

"His voice. He sounds old." And not quite human, which she wouldn't dare tell Leah, given her friend's vivid imagination.

"A dirty old man, then."

"Leah! He was a friend of my father's!"

"Even vampires must have friends." She held up a hand to stave off more protests. "Fine. I still say he's weird."

"Eccentric."

Leah made a face. "What do you tell people who call here and insist on speaking with the company's president personally?"

"That, if I can't help them, I'll have him return their call. And he must do that because they rarely call back and give me grief."

"I still say he's a vampire with the hots for you."

"You and Jimmy need to stop watching *Buffy the Vampire Slayer* DVDs."

"Hey, that show's a classic."

"Did you come here to harass me or is there a purpose behind this interruption?"

"What interruption? You should have quit an hour

ago and you were locking up for the day after giving that police detective hell."

"They aren't even listening to me, Leah."

"I know. I heard some of your conversation at lunchtime, remember? Your cousin and his wife are satisfied with the police report. So are your aunt and uncle and everyone else. And it's been months. Are you sure your father was murdered?"

"Not you, too."

"I just mean the police must have a reason to think—"

"Lots of them. But tell me this. Why haven't they identified the other body yet?"

"Because his fingerprints aren't on file anywhere? Look, Kelly, harassing everyone who knew your dad isn't helping anyone."

"What else can I do?" Kelly turned away from the pity in Leah's large brown eyes. She didn't want to be angry with her, too. "Are you here for a reason?"

"Yes. I wanted to see if you'd like to come to the Golden Goose with Jimmy and me tonight. They have a new band playing."

"Thanks, but pass."

"Your dad wouldn't want you to mope around."

"I am not moping around."

"Okay, poor word choice. But you have to move on and you're never going to meet anyone sitting here in this secluded office all day."

"I met you and Jimmy, didn't I?"

"Because I work next door. I'm talking about the male half of the species."

"What's Jimmy?"

"I've asked that question more than once."

Kelly managed a smile. Leah could be annoying, but Kelly found her fun to be around and she knew her friend meant well.

"I'm serious. You need to get out and meet people," Leah continued.

"There's Fred—"

"Fifty years old and married."

"He's barely forty-five," Kelly corrected, turning off the computer, "and his wife is really nice. She's the one who sends in those brownies you like so much."

"Okay, I do not mean to alienate the goddess of brownies, but my point is valid. And don't you dare mention Riley because we both know your architect is happily gay. You need to get out and meet people your own age—" she held up a hand to stave off the rebuttal "—who don't speak English as a second language and don't consider a tool pack around their waist a necessary fashion statement. Have some fun, for a change."

Shaking her head, Kelly continued clearing her desk and neatening the office. "Haven't you ever heard three's a crowd? Maybe Jimmy would like some one-on-one time with you."

"Let me worry about Jimmy. He gets…" Abruptly, Leah's eyes widened. "Ohmygod. You're going to try again, aren't you? You're going to see if you can catch the vampire when he rises tonight and comes in to check his mail."

Sometimes, Leah was entirely too discerning for comfort. "Will you stop with the vampire stuff, already?"

"You are, aren't you? Hey, you want some help?"

"No and no. Mr. Prince is a nice man. A bit eccentric—" her friend snorted "—but a good partner. I have a lot of autonomy and I enjoy the challenge. If he wants to be all mysterious, that's his prerogative. Custom Concepts is building a solid reputation for creating individual houses in a tight market and I'm going to see it continues to do that."

"While the Midnight Prince gets all the credit."

That was a too close to the truth. Even though she ran everything, James Prince did get most of the credit, at least, on paper. "Don't you have someplace you have to be that isn't here?"

"Okay. But if you come in tomorrow morning wearing a high neckline or a scarf I'm going to want to see the bite marks."

"Go home. Go to the Golden Goose. Just go away. And say hi to Jimmy for me. I have to lock up now."

"Spoilsport." Leah opened the front door and paused. "But if you do see him, I want details."

"Go!"

With an infectious grin, her friend scooted out the door. Kelly turned the deadbolt and shut off the main lights, leaving only the designated night-light on overhead. Double-checking to be sure the coffee pot was off and clean, she set the opened mail on the desk in James Prince's office and stared at the mostly empty room.

Other than a simple desk with a computer and a printer/fax combination, the small room boasted a leather chair, a set of matching file cabinets and little else. There were no pictures, no mirrors, nothing at all of a personal nature. The walls were primer white and the floor was bare concrete. This was the only office that had no windows. It was also the only one that had a door leading directly outside.

"At least there isn't a coffin in the corner." Mentally, she chided herself. Leah was starting to rub off on her in the worst possible way.

The keys to this place had been delivered to her cousin only days after her initial conversation with James Prince. Her cousin hadn't paid any attention to the man who'd dropped them off. All he'd remembered was that the delivery person had been an older man with gray hair. James Prince had subsequently apologized for missing her, but she was pretty sure he'd deliberately selected a time when she wasn't home to show up. He seemed bent on remaining a man of mystery and it was driving her crazy.

As much as she tried to be okay with this strange work situation, she wasn't. Leah was right, she was planning to lie in wait for the puzzling man again tonight. But unlike last Tuesday night, this time, she'd do it from outside the warehouse.

She'd come to the conclusion James Prince was probably deformed in some way that left him reluctant to meet with people. While she wanted to respect his need for privacy, she was determined to talk to him face to face. Despite hours of research, she could find no trace of anyone named James Prince who would have enough money to casually sink thousands into a venture like this one. Kelly didn't want to look a gift horse in the mouth. However, she also didn't want to find out she was partners with the mafia or worse.

James Prince had claimed he had been out of the country when her father died. What if he hadn't been? What if he and her father had had a falling out? Just because James Prince sounded like a nice person didn't make him one.

Kelly sighed. She wanted answers to some of the wild conjectures she'd come up with regarding the man. His signature was bold and round, a firm sure hand. But that was the only written thing she'd ever seen from him. His notes to her were always done on the computer. And what totally creeped her out was the absence of fingerprints in his office. She kept everything neat and polished, yet there had never been a single print on the well-oiled desk or the pen he used to sign papers. Either he wore gloves or he didn't have any fingerprints. She wasn't sure which thought worried her most.

The warehouse itself was large and spacious, yet the offices showed signs of having been hastily assembled. Every stick of furniture was new down to the pens and pencils. The first time she'd walked in, there had been printed sticky notes on each door indicating which rooms belonged to which person. Kelly wasn't sure whether it was that he'd made the choices without consulting her first or that he'd made the same choices she would have made, given the opportunity, but this, too, had gotten under her skin.

A small receptionist's office sat near the main entrance. A waiting area across from it held comfortable chairs, a small couch, a coffee table and two end tables with a rack of magazines. Behind that wall was the open bay for storing equipment.

Next to the front office was a room with a good-sized conference table and a small office for the architect to use when he was there. Her office was in the corner along the back hall. Next came a surprisingly generous bathroom, a storage closet and his office.

It nearly broke her heart when she'd first walked into her designated office and found a large vase of mixed flowers on her desk and a series of photographs hanging on one wall. The were all of her father—laughing, a hard hat perched on his head, sitting at his desk in the old trailer, out on a job site, even one of dad and her mother, smiling at each other and obviously in love. But the central photo, her favorite, was of her and her dad taken the day she received her MBA, only weeks before he died. It wasn't posed and she had no idea who had taken the picture, but her father was beaming and she was smiling proudly back at him. A happy moment out of time that never failed to bring a sense of regret and longing whenever she gazed at it.

The walls might have been hastily assembled but someone had paid attention to the details in every room except   James Prince's office. His was sparsely furnished, which for her made sense since it appeared he was never there any longer than it took him to sign a few papers. The heavy steel door led outside onto the darkest, most remote part of the parking area. As he'd told her, James Prince took his privacy seriously.

Kelly wondered what he did for a day job that he could afford all new equipment, including the two brand-new trucks parked in the lot, not to mention the rent on this place. It depressed her to think about it because she suspected she might never be able to afford to buy him out. That didn't mean she wasn't going to try. She didn't like being partners with an invisible man.

Several times now she had tried to catch him coming or going. She'd even spent the entire night in her office last Tuesday. Unfortunately, despite her best efforts to stay awake, she'd dozed off. She woke to find a message blinking on her computer screen telling her to go home and get some rest. He'd come and gone and she'd never heard a thing.

Tonight, she was going to try something different. Tonight, she would leave her car two warehouse buildings over and walk back. Obviously, Mr. Prince used the door to his office so she'd found the perfect place to sit in the grass near an overgrown cluster of bushes. From there, she had a view of the door without being seen, herself. When he arrived tonight, she'd be waiting. She would not fall asleep this time. She had caffeine pills to make sure of that. She'd already warned Fred and their young receptionist, Tammy, that she probably wouldn't be in until late afternoon the following day. Being a Friday, things would be slow, anyhow.

She went to dinner first and did a little shopping, knowing he never came before dark. But walking back to her selected spot, she realized how isolated the area was at night. This was probably a stupid idea. That thought grew to a certainty the longer she sat on the damp ground, feeling colder and more chilled by the hour. By 4:00 a.m. she knew he wasn't coming.

There was no way he could know she was sitting here, yet somehow he had. The thought made her shiver. Did he have her office bugged or was that idea a sign of total paranoia?

Stiff, cold and discouraged, she stopped hunching in her jacket, picked up her blanket and Thermos and trudged back to her car. He'd outsmarted her once again. Tomorrow, or rather today, she was going to search her office for listening devices and she didn't care if that was paranoid.

Wearily, she drove to her dad's apartment. Her own stuff was still in storage. Soon, she'd have to decide if she wanted to keep his place or find another apartment of her own. It didn't matter, really. Her dad hadn't been living in this one long enough to create any memories. And right now was no time to make life-altering decisions.

Early morning commuters were beginning to stir, though dawn hadn't quite broken through the fall of night. The parking lot was still and empty as she entered the apartment building.

She didn't bother turning on lights inside. Exhaustion tugged at her. She shrugged out of her jacket and hung it up. She needed to get out of her damp clothing, take a shower and go to bed, but, despite feeling tired, the caffeine pill had done its job all too well. Tired did not mean sleepy. Pulling a bottle of water from the refrigerator, she crossed to the sliding-glass door and stared out at the night.

If she decided to say here, the first thing she needed to do was buy drapes for the windows. The apartment was like a goldfish bowl. Her dad had only moved in a few weeks before he was killed and he'd never gotten around to drapes or pictures for the walls.

Pain washed over her. The night felt as empty as her heart. She missed him so much.

There was a flash of movement at the edge of the patio. Frozen, Kelly stared at the spot. A skinny gray cat stepped onto the concrete patio and looked straight at her. Her tensed muscles relaxed.

The animal had been hanging around for a couple of weeks now. The building didn't allow pets and there were no houses close enough for the cat to consider this part of its territory. Besides, the little thing was too thin to have a loving home. She hated to see any animal go hungry, so with only a little reservation, she'd bought a bag of cat food and began feeding it.

She'd debated calling animal control, but fear that they might put the poor thing to sleep had kept her from making the call. The cat was so friendly, it had obviously been someone's pet once.

"All right, cat. Give me a minute."

Kelly went back in the kitchen and poured some dry cat food into a disposable bowl. Opening the sliding-glass door, she stepped onto the patio. The cat appeared, swished its tail imperiously and mewed at her.

That was new. Normally, the cat made no sound.

"What's the matter, kitty?"

It took two steps away from the patio, stopped and gazed back at her with what could only be called impatience.

"You want me to follow you? I thought only dogs did that."

She'd heard of animals acting oddly when they needed help. Maybe it had a litter of kittens nearby. She'd seen that it was a female when it rolled over to invite a belly rub.

The cat ran toward the tree line at the top of the slope and stopped, looking back as if to say *hurry up*.

Maybe if she hadn't been so tired, or if she'd given it a little more thought, she wouldn't have gone any farther, but this being such a quiet neighborhood, Kelly didn't give it any thought at all. She followed the cat up the slope until she saw something move at the base of the sweeping cedar trees that lined the knoll.

"Oh!"

Not a litter of kittens. A man.

He was trying to rise, obviously hurt. Kelly hesitated, her instinct to flee tempered by a need to help. "Stay still," she called to him. "I'm going to go call for help."

"No."

The soft command raised the hair on the back of her arms. She backed up a pace, unsure now if he was injured or drunk. He wiped at his face. Her eyes were adjusted enough to the dark to see the gesture left a smear of something behind. Blood?

The stray cat wound itself around her legs. She ignored the animal and stared at the man. He was tall and lean with broad shoulders. There was a tear in the sleeve of his jacket. Another rip ran from the zipper to a spot just above his waistline.

"You're hurt. You shouldn't move."

"I'm okay."

Obviously, he was far from okay. "It's better when a lie is at least marginally believable, you know," she pointed out, trying to sound calm.

His lips curved as he stood there swaying. "I didn't want you to panic."

That decided her. She stepped around the cat and moved closer. "You'd better lean on me."

"You might be right."

He leaned a considerable amount of weight on

her shoulder to steady himself. She staggered, nearly taking them both down. "Sorry."

"I'm too heavy."

"Yeah, I say the same thing every morning when I step on the scale."

A snort and a sound that might have been a chuckle rumbled forth. His injured hand went to his stomach where the other tear had opened his jacket.

"Look, you're really hurt. This is a bad idea. Sit back down and let me go inside and call an ambulance."

"No. I'm fine."

"Liar. We'll never make it down the hill."

He didn't waste breath on a reply. He stumbled in the direction of her father's apartment. In retrospect, that was the last place she wanted him to go, but there wasn't much choice unless she squirmed free of his iron grip and let him fall face down in the grass again.

"You could just roll me the rest of the way down," he offered.

She liked his calm, offbeat sense of humor. "We'll try walking first."

Somehow, they made it, even when he tripped and nearly fell over the concrete pad of the patio. Breathing hard, she got him inside where he collapsed onto one of her father's sturdy dining-room chairs.

"Wasn't much of a fight," he agreed with a wry smile.

"Not funny."

"No. It wasn't, but you should see the other guy."

"Someone else is out there, hurt?"

"Oh, I managed to hurt him, but he took off. My mistake was trying to chase him up that hill."

"We need to call the police."

"No." He started to sway. "Reporters."

"What?" Was he delirious or was he saying he was a reporter? "Look, mister, I don't care if you are a reporter. You're bleeding and we have to get you some help."

He reached back for the chair and practically fell onto the seat, still holding the telephone's handset. "I'll call a friend."

Only he couldn't seem to make his fingers work.

Abruptly, the phone fell from his hand, bounced off the tabletop and slid across the carpeting. He dropped his head on his good arm and, for a second, she thought he'd stopped breathing.

"Hey! Don't you dare die!"

"No," he agreed, but didn't lift his head.

She started forward and nearly screamed as something brushed against her leg. A pair of luminous wide eyes gazed up at her. The stray cat gave a soft mew.

"Jeez, cat! You scared me! What are you doing in here?"

And what did it matter? Dawn was cracking open the night and they were still sitting here in full view of anyone who cared to look.

The man raised his head. For the first time, Kelly realized his lower lip was bleeding. A fistfight that had turned into a knife fight?

What did it matter? He needed medical attention.

"Bathroom?" he asked.

She'd always been a sucker for the underdog. Despite his size and his wounds, his sense of humor was distinctly nonthreatening.

"Down the hall on the right."

Getting them both away from this uncovered patio window was probably a good idea. He pushed down on the table and made it to his feet, but she wasn't sure he could make it down the short hall to the bathroom on his own.

"Here, lean on me again."

"This is starting to become a habit. Thanks."

"It had better not."

His easy acceptance of her help surprised her. There wasn't time to think about that as they crossed the short distance to the small bathroom. Kelly was relieved the two-bedroom apartment wasn't very big because she was pretty sure he wouldn't be going much farther, even with help.

Up close, that faint trace of a light, spicy aftershave mingled with a stronger scent of alcohol. Combined with the coppery scent of blood, she revised the fight up a notch to a drunken brawl. He didn't seem drunk, but maybe the staggering was due to alcohol and not his injuries. She almost hoped that was the case.

He stepped inside and she flipped on the light, getting her first real view of the man. She sucked in an involuntary breath. He was incredibly good-looking. Thick black unruly hair, gorgeous blue eyes and the features of a Hollywood leading man. His face even looked vaguely familiar. She'd seen him somewhere before.

"Towel?"

Distracted by the question, Kelly indicated the rack to his right. "These are clean. I put them out this morning before I left for work."

He stared at the fluffy pale yellow towels and back at her. "I'll get blood on them."

"Oh. I thought you needed to... Never mind. Look, mister, you really need medical attention." In the light, the amount of blood was frightening.

"No." His eyes held her gaze.

"You've been knifed."

"Noticed that, did you? I'll live."

"Good plan, but I'd rather hear it from a doctor."

He shook his head. "Sorry. No doctor."

While he might have been drinking, he wasn't

drunk now. That gaze was far too alert and aware, not to mention filled with steely determination. Of course, being stabbed would probably sober anyone up fast.

"Okay. If you don't want to go to the hospital, I can't make you—unless you fall down unconscious. Then all bets are off."

He gave her a lopsided, boyish grin that rippled right through her.

"Deal."

He waited patiently. Kelly sighed. "Okay. I know I'm going to regret this, but don't move. I'll get the first-aid kit."

"Thank you."

"Don't thank me, yet. I've had grown men run from the sight of me with a first-aid kit in my hands."

That smile flashed again. "I promise I won't run."

The look in his eyes was deeply unsettling. Warm, kind—a puppy dog with bright blue eyes might regard her the same way.

"You say that now," she agreed shakily.

She dropped her gaze from his face with haste and indicated the commode. "Sit down. I'll be right back."

Kelly didn't wait to see if he obeyed. She pulled the first-aid kit from the hall linen closet and snatched up several of her dad's older towels. Her mystery man was still standing at the sink as she dumped everything on the vanity.

"Sit down before you fall over. I'll be right back."

Hurrying to the kitchen, she pulled a cold pack from the freezer without turning on the lights and nearly tripped over the gray cat again. The animal was all but invisible in the dim light. It stropped her legs and mewed up at her.

"Oh, for… All right, I agree you're a hero, but he's the one who owes you, not me. Here." She filled another plastic bowl with food, spilling the vile-smelling crunchies all over the floor in her rush. Filling a second bowl with water, she slopped both on the floor before rushing back to the bathroom with the ice pack.

He was wringing out one of the washcloths, having removed his coat and his shirt to reveal a lean, muscled chest with a light sprinkling of dark hair. Kelly froze in the doorway. She'd grown up around construction sites with bare-chested males running around much of the time so the sight of a man's chest, even one as superb as his, shouldn't cause her brain to fuzz. Yet, for a second, that's exactly what it seemed to do.

More likely, it was the sight of all that blood oozing from the nasty-looking cut that made her knees feel weak. The jagged slit started low on his left side and tapered away to more of a scratch near the center of his chest.

"He tried to stab me, but I moved," he explained, following her gaze.

"Who tried to stab you?"

"The guy with the knife."

"Here I thought it was the cat."

"What cat?"

Kelly shook her head. "Do you know him?"

"The cat?"

"The man with the knife."

A flash of anger. "Not yet."

"O-kay. That sounds very vigilante."

He didn't respond, nor did he look contrite.

"How many of them were there?"

Ruefully, he held up a single finger.

"Ouch."

"Yes," he agreed. "Not my best moment."

She handed him the cold pack. "Hold this against your lip. It'll help reduce the swelling. I need to look at this cut. You were lucky you were wearing that jacket. It protected you some, but your stomach could probably use a couple of stitches."

"Pass."

"It may scar."

"I'll take that chance. Just slap a couple of butterfly closures on it. It'll be fine."

"If you say so. Mind telling me what happened?"

"He wanted my wallet. I objected."

Kelly frowned. "Was it worth it?"

The lopsided smile appeared again. "I still have my wallet."

"Uh-huh."

"You don't approve."

"We all have our priorities."

Briskly rinsing out the wet washcloth, Kelly perched on the commode. He turned to face her and she tried not to think about how intimate this was as she carefully dabbed at the clotting blood. He was all muscle and taut skin around the angry tear.

"I'll tape this, but you really should have this cut looked at by someone who knows what they're doing. Hand me the peroxide."

He did and their fingers brushed. His hand was so much larger than hers that, for an awkward moment, she stared. Funny how a thing like that could remind her of her femininity even at a time like this. She shook off the thought. His fingernails were surprisingly clean and neatly manicured. She was used to seeing work-roughened hands, not smooth, long-fingered hands like these.

She forced herself to focus on her task. "This is going to sting, but we don't know how dirty that knife was, so…"

He inhaled sharply as she poured the peroxide into the cut. "I can see why grown men fear you."

"I did warn you."

"I'll pay more attention next time."

Taking a tube of antiseptic ointment, she blotted the running foam with one hand and unscrewed the cap with the other. "You make a habit of this?"

"No. Ow! That stuff really burns."

"It's supposed to. What is it about grown men that they can face down a man with a knife, but they're afraid of a doctor and his needles?"

"Genetic defect?"

Without looking up, she knew he was smiling that devastating smile of his again. Quickly, she applied ointment to the area. Her gaze fell on the waistband of his pants for the first time. No belt. Not even any belt loops. The black material proclaimed them dress slacks and there was a narrow banded stripe of satin running down either side of the leg on the outside. Kelly was no maven of men's fashion but she'd swear they looked like they were made to go with a tuxedo.

"You didn't just get married, did you?"

"No."

Looking up she met the puzzled surprise in his eyes. They were intriguing eyes. Inviting eyes. And she really, really needed to get some sleep.

"Why did you ask if I just got married?"

"Your pants."

Her gaze flew to his hand. No wedding ring, but he had a pricey-looking gold watch on his left wrist. His polished dress shoes also looked expensive. No wonder someone had tried to take his wallet.

Why had this man been running around her neighborhood in half a tuxedo at this hour? On the verge of asking, Kelly decided she didn't want to know the answer.

"Never mind." She just wanted him cleaned up and out of her apartment so she could get at least a couple of hours of sleep before she had to go back to work.

"I'm finished. We should probably run some strapping tape around your middle to hold these bandages in place."

"Okay."

She glanced up and saw weary acceptance. The adrenaline rush was fading and so was he. She needed to get him taped and out of here before he went face down on her.

Winding the tape around his firm, naked torso would have felt entirely too intimate if Kelly had let herself think about it, so she didn't. He stood still with his eyes mostly closed while she wrapped and taped the area down tight and turned her attention to his arm. This cut was also deeper than she would have liked, but it had already clotted closed, so she cleaned and bandaged it without comment. He stood stoically at first, then began to sway.

"Hey! You aren't passing out on me, are you?"

"Just tired."

Kelly hurried. "Stay with me another couple of minutes, okay? Then you can leave."

The sway became more pronounced.

"I hate to be a bother," his eyes closed completely, "but would you mind if I lie down for a minute?"

"Here?" Her protest sounded like a squeak. He couldn't stay here. She didn't even know who he was. She didn't want to know who he was. She wanted him gone.

But, while that might be what she wanted, he was in no shape to take himself anywhere—nor be any sort of a threat to her. There was no way he was staying on his feet much longer. At least, she'd changed the sheets in her father's bedroom after her cousin had left.

"Okay, lean on me."

Tired eyes flashed open. "I can walk."

"No offense, but I doubt it."

The curve of his lips didn't quite make it into a smile, but he stumbled across the hall to her father's room under his own steam and steadied himself against the wall.

"Can you stand while I turn down the bed?"

Kelly didn't wait for an answer. She raced to the bed and peeled back the covers. When she turned around, he had toed off his shoes and was fumbling for the button at his waistband.

He was going to take off his pants?

"What are you doing?" she yelped.

"Don't want to get blood on the sheets."

"Oh."

Before she could protest further, her brain stopped at the overly loud sound of his zipper. He skimmed the pants down past slim hips, a pair of dark briefs and nicely muscled legs. The pants pooled at his feet, but stepping out of them seemed beyond his ability. If she didn't help, he'd never make the bed. He was seconds away from falling where he stood.

Reluctantly, Kelly moved to steady him. With exaggerated care, he stepped clear of the pants and staggered toward the bed.

"Thank you."

"You're welcome."

He sank down and his eyes closed.

"Hey!"

He didn't move. There wasn't so much as a flicker behind his eyelids.

Chapter Three

What if he had a concussion? What if he had internal injuries? What if he died here?

Kelly waited, holding her breath until the rise and fall of his chest told her he was still alive.

"Great. Just great." She glared at the unconscious man on her father's bed and tried not to imagine the worst. He could still die. And, if he didn't, what was she going to do with him come morning?

Who was he?

What was he doing here?

A sane woman would call the police right now—or at least an ambulance. Why wasn't she doing either one? She'd always thought of herself as sane and practical, yet she knew she wasn't going to make any calls.

Sighing, Kelly debated for several seconds and then removed his socks, covered him, picked up his pants and carried everything back into the bathroom. There was even blood on one of his socks. By morning, his clothing would be too stiff with dried blood to put back on and his pants and jacket weren't the sort of things she could just dump in the washer.

Looking down, she realized her own top was stained in his blood, as well. She sighed again as she stripped it off and began running cold water in the tub. If she rinsed everything now he could put his clothes back on and leave when he woke.

Kelly removed a cell phone, a set of keys and his wallet from the pocket of his pants. He'd nearly died to protect this bit of incredibly soft leather. After a moment's hesitation, she decided it wouldn't be prying to look inside. She'd earned the right to at least know his name.

Dumping the clothes in the tub she sat down on the commode to open the wallet. The wad of cash inside started her heart thumping. No wonder he'd wanted to protect his wallet. He must be a drug dealer, after all. Who else carried this sort of cash around?

Kelly stared at the name on his driver's license and got her answer. Reece Maddox.

For a second she was pretty sure she stopped breathing while the impossible sank in. Reece Maddox was lying on her father's bed. The same Reece Maddox who frequently made the society columns escorting this famous starlet or that famous model to the sort of parties people like her only read about in magazines and newspapers. The same Reece Maddox whose family's line of clothing made money as easily as breathing. *That* Reece Maddox was right *here* in her father's apartment.

She'd just undressed an internationally famous playboy. Leah would die.

What was she thinking? Never mind Leah, what was Reece Maddox doing inside her suburban Maryland apartment?

No wonder he hadn't wanted her to call the police or an ambulance. And that's what he'd meant when he'd mentioned reporters. Calling the police would bring reporters out from under every rock in town. Could there be a bigger gossip story? Reece Maddox in a knife fight in suburbia.

Kelly closed her eyes and groaned out loud. Opening her eyes, she stared at the plain white tile around the tub. What was she supposed to do now?

The irony of the situation didn't escape her. Most women would kill to be in her position. She wished someone else were. This was not good. This was very, very bad. If the press connected her to Reece Maddox she wouldn't have a moment's privacy. Her life and her father's murder would make headlines once more, only this time his death would be spread all over the world in the most titillating fashion imaginable. Her father would be internationally labeled a drunk who died in a brawl and a fire. She'd never get anyone to listen to the truth then. The press wouldn't care. They certainly wouldn't take up her cause. They'd only be interested in smearing dirt all over Reece Maddox and they'd use her and her father in the process.

She reached over and turned off the water swallowing panic. Reece was right. She no longer wanted to call anyone. She wanted him to wake up and sneak away as quietly as he'd appeared.

The small gray cat padded into the room. Crossing to the tub, she rose up to peer over the side.

"This is your fault. You just had to play hero, didn't you?"

The animal ignored her. Satisfied there was nothing in the tub worth her time she sat back and began to groom herself.

"Don't you have somewhere to go?"

The cat didn't deign to look at her.

Kelly set the wallet on the back of the toilet and stood. The cat fled when she bent over the tub and began rinsing out the sopping wet clothes. She hadn't meant for them to get quite this wet. She'd been distracted by his wallet and his name. Especially his name. Kelly exhaled shakily. Too late for regrets.

She should have dumped everything in her tiny washing machine, after all. The stained and torn jacket and shirt were history no matter what she did. He'd never be able to wear them. She'd have to offer him something of her father's. While tall like Reece, her dad was heavier.

Had been heavier.

Tears threatened without warning. She swallowed hard at what felt like boulders in the back of her throat. Her loss caught her like this at unexpected moments, usually at night when she was tired. She did not want to think about how much she wished her father were here right this minute. He would have known what to do.

But Eugene O'Donnell hadn't raised his daughter to be a wimp. He'd raised her to do what needed to be done. She pushed back grief and, by the time she finished hanging everything to drip dry over the shower and neatened the bathroom, the last of her energy was gone. Stripping off the rest of her clothes, she fell into bed wondering if she wouldn't have been better off if Reece had been some sort of drug dealer or criminal, after all.

PAIN PULLED REECE from the comfort zone of sleep to find a small gray cat snuggled on the pillow beside him sound asleep. Afternoon sun poured into the simple bedroom past the dusty venetian blinds. The burning pain in his abdomen and his arm had combined with aches in other places he didn't know he'd injured to set up a chorus of complaints.

"If you add insult to that by having fleas, cat, I'm going to wring your furry little neck."

The cat opened surprisingly green eyes, apparently decided Reece wasn't serious and went back to sleep. Reece lay still, listening hard. The apartment was utterly silent. Had Kelly left him here? The unlikely possibility brought him upright on the bed, sending the small cat leaping for the safety of the floor. Across the hall, the toilet flushed. Reece closed his eyes in relief. Kelly was here and she was safe. Now it was up to him to keep her that way.

Reece lay back down quickly. The door to his room was wide-open. The minute she stepped from the bathroom she would see him and he wasn't ready to have a conversation just yet. Feigning sleep, he listened hard. Kelly left the bathroom and Reece sensed her standing over him a few seconds later. After what felt like a very long moment she crossed the room to open the closet.

Risking discovery, he peered through his eyelashes. Kelly had her back to him, staring at the clothes hanging inside. After some hesitation, she selected a pair of men's pants and a shirt. Reece closed his eyes before she turned and set the garments on the end of the bed. Once more he sensed her looking at him.

Before they talked again he needed a believable story to explain how he'd come to be outside her apartment at four-thirty in the morning. He could hardly tell her he'd been waiting to be sure she made it home safely so he could drive over to the warehouse and take care of business.

The last thing he'd expected was to confront someone trying to get into her apartment.

Reece was glad now that he'd taken the precaution of distorting his voice on the phone whenever he'd called, otherwise she might have recognized him as James Prince.

And what she knew, others could learn.

Reece lay there thinking, long after he knew she'd left the room. Only when he heard the shower start up across the hall, did he move. It hurt. More than he expected. With a grunt of pain and a wince he sat up and looked around for his pants. Gone. All of his things were gone except his dress shoes, which were sitting near the door where he'd left them.

Reece swallowed a moment of panic. He stared at the clothes she'd left on the end of the bed. Gene's clothes. The image of his robust features tugged forth a host of memories that brought a sudden lump to the back of Reece's throat.

Gene was dead because of him and Reece was oddly reluctant to dress in his friend's clothes. They'd be too big, anyhow. Gene had been heavier, broader through the chest and more muscular. Just thinking of him caused a physical pang of both guilt and regret.

Reece had never been close to his own father. Gene had been a surrogate in many ways as well as his friend and confidant. They hadn't been able to spend nearly as much time together as Reece would have liked, but Gene's death left an empty void nothing else could fill. Reece could only imagine what it was like for Kelly.

He shoved aside old memories and got gingerly to his feet to take a look around. What had she done with his pants? His wallet! Even his cell phone was missing.

He stepped into the hall and the bathroom door swung wide.

A wash of steamy air drifted out to surround Kelly like a halo. She wore a baggy white terry-cloth robe belted securely at an intriguingly narrow waist. Her hair was covered in a yellow turban made from one of the towels he remembered from the night before. Dainty feet were bare and slim and nicely shaped legs disappeared beneath the hem of the robe. Her face had a dewy, fresh-scrubbed look that reminded him of the way she'd looked in a picture her father had shown him of her at sixteen after pitching a no-hitter for the girl's high-school softball team.

Okay, there'd been grime on one cheek that day and her hair had been caught up in a ponytail, but right this second, it was easy enough to imagine what this lovely woman had been like as that sixteen-year-old girl.

"Oh!" Her gaze skated down his chest, returning rapidly to fix itself on a point near his left ear as her rosy complexion deepened.

"Sorry. I didn't mean to startle you."

"That's okay." She sounded breathless. "I didn't mean to wake you."

"You didn't. Where are my pants?"

Her cheeks reddened even more.

"I'm fairly certain I was wearing some when we first met."

The turban slid down to cover her eyes. She shoved it up distractedly without looking at him. "They're still wet."

"Wet?"

Delicate shoulders rose and fell. "I only meant to rinse out the blood, but I wasn't paying attention and they clogged the drain. The tub filled with water and they haven't had time to dry."

As she fussed with the towel rather than look at him, he decided that almost made sense.

"Did you put them in the dryer?"

Her eyes shot to his, appalled by the suggestion. "You can't put tuxedo pants in a dryer!"

"So what did you do with them?"

"I hung them in the kitchen while I took my shower. I left you some things of my father's on the end of the bed."

Her gaze skimmed down his chest and zoomed

back to his face while the delicate pink suffusing her cheeks ran together with her freckles. Reece remembered he was standing inches away from her, dressed in nothing but a pair of briefs and a couple of bandages.

"And my socks? I'm pretty sure I was wearing them when I fell asleep."

Her cheeks continued to flame. She lowered her gaze to his collarbone. "There was blood on one of them, too. I didn't want to get it on the sheets."

"Of course." He'd stripped down to his briefs in front of her, so why did her removing his socks seem so intimate?

"You didn't by any chance wash my wallet, too, did you?"

That snapped her out of her stunned state. Eyes of blue crystal glared up at him.

"Of course not. I left your wallet in the bathroom on the back of the toilet along with your cell phone and your keys. Your money's all there. You can count it. I didn't take anything."

"Hey." He gripped her arm gently when she would have brushed past. A slight quiver ran through her. "I didn't mean to sound accusatory, although, I confess I was a little worried." He let his lips curve upward. "We'd be here all day ironing the money."

She blinked in confusion. Her lips opened and

closed again soundlessly. Finally, she summoned a glare. "You don't believe in banks or credit cards?"

"Most places still accept cash with proper ID," he teased, dropping his hands. Instantly, she moved away. She didn't return his smile.

"Excuse me. I need to get dressed."

She crossed to the other bedroom and shut the door. Reece hesitated. Maybe he should apologize for teasing her. Or not. The best thing he could do was leave as quickly and unobtrusively as possible. Kelly O'Donnell was entirely too likeable.

The bathroom was still steamy from her shower and smelled of some light, feminine fragrance. He eyed the shower with longing, but thought better of it at a twinge from his cuts. The bastard had been quick with that knife last night. If Reece hadn't had martial arts training, he'd be dead right now.

He took some satisfaction in the knowledge that he'd at least broken his attacker's arm. Reece hadn't expected the knife. Really stupid of him. He'd been lucky all around and he knew it. That sobering thought accompanied him into her small kitchen where he found his clothing on hangers dangling from various cupboard pulls. She was right. Everything was too wet to wear.

Reece located her small dryer and tossed the clothes inside, figuring they were a lost cause, anyhow. The shirt and jacket didn't even qualify as rags. Wearing them into his apartment building would raise more than eyebrows, but there was no point letting them drip all over her floor. He returned to the bathroom in search of a razor.

After washing and shaving, he undid the tape and examined the ugly red gash on his stomach. The wound had bled through while he slept and hurt like the devil. While it wasn't all that deep, maybe Kelly had been right about the stitches. Still, a scar was the least of his worries. He set about retaping everything from the first-aid kit she'd left sitting out.

She was still in her bedroom when he returned to the kitchen and started her coffeepot. As soon as the noise of her hair dryer stopped, he grabbed his now damp and ruined pants from the dryer and struggled into them, a difficult feat considering how shriveled they were. He got them mostly zipped before he gave up the struggle. She'd seen him in less.

He'd finished pouring coffee into two mugs when Kelly appeared in a pair of jeans with a radiophone clipped to an empty belt loop. Her long hair was bunched on top of her head in a no-nonsense style. A pair of crystal earrings that he knew had been a present from her father dangled from her earlobes. A long-sleeved, high-necked, dark brown pullover completed the outfit.

She looked casual, competent and all business. Her gaze shot to his bare stomach and the bandages there. "You should have had stitches."

He shrugged, handed her the mug he'd doctored with more creamer than coffee and smiled. "Too late."

She didn't even glance at the liquid. "Mr. Maddox—"

So she had looked through his wallet. "Reece," he corrected.

She held his gaze. "I know you don't want the press to get hold of this story—"

"Do you?"

She blanched. "No!"

"Thanks."

She flushed once more. "You're an international playboy!"

"You make me sound like the plague. Don't believe everything you read."

"I don't," she assured him. "But I really don't want my name linked with yours."

"Again with the thanks."

Her cheeks were cherry, but she didn't look the least bit contrite. "Sorry if I'm tromping on your ego—"

"Tromping on it, stomping on it and burying it six feet under," he assured her.

She turned her gaze on her coffee mug and froze.

Blue eyes flashed to his. There was the start of fear in their depths.

"How did you know how I take my coffee?"

Too late, Reece realized his mistake. Her father had once told him she took her coffee with so much creamer there was barely room for the coffee itself. The memory had stayed with him. But Reece Maddox shouldn't have known that.

"Did I get it wrong?" He tried to look contrite while his pulse raced. "You had the economy-sized half-and-half in your refrigerator and not a whole lot of other stuff so I figured..." He shrugged. "Sorry. I shouldn't have assumed. Dump it out and I'll pour you a fresh cup."

"No. It's fine." But she didn't relax and the wariness remained as she stared at him.

"My sister always told me my impulsiveness would get me in trouble."

"Like last night?"

"Technically, it was this morning." He wished she'd loosen her death grip on the mug. "What happened wasn't my fault. A case of being in the wrong place at the wrong time."

"What were you doing here?"

"You don't have to make it sound like I was caught inside a bank vault."

She wasn't diverted. "This isn't the sort of neighborhood someone like you hangs out in."

"Someone like me?"

"Yes. Someone rich, famous and as out of place here as a snake on a wedding cake."

"Now there's an image," he stalled. "Look, Kelly—"

She stilled again. "How did you know my name?"

Mentally, Reece swore. Outwardly, he strove for calm. "I saw it on a piece of mail on your dining-room table," he improvised.

She glanced at the multitude of papers spread all over the table and he prayed there was something there addressed to her.

When she would have started in that direction, the wall phone trilled behind her, making them both jump. Kelly set her coffee on the counter with visibly wobbly fingers. Never taking suspicious eyes from him, she reached for the phone.

He knew better. Mistakes like these could get a person killed. *Had* gotten a person killed. And, if that guy last night had been just a little faster, Reece might have been added to the tally.

"What? Tammy, slow down."

Even from where he stood, Reece could hear the shrill pitch of the young woman's voice if not the actual words. Reece knew Tammy Messner was the nineteen-year-old receptionist Kelly had recently hired.

"Which site?" Kelly gripped the receiver more tightly. "How bad?"

Reece stared alertly.

"Okay, take it easy. I was on my way in but I'll go there first. Call Fred. Tell him he can get me on the two-way. Better yet, I'll call him. Just calm down, Tammy. I'm sure Louis will be fine. Accidents happen all the time in this business. Sit tight. I'll call you when I know something."

She hung up, her distracted expression worried. "I have to go. One of my men was injured. Is there somewhere I can drop you?"

He nearly asked who'd been hurt and bit it back in time. Reece Maddox didn't know Kelly ran a construction company, either, let alone the names of her employees.

"I was going to call a friend to come pick me up," he lied. His car was parked on the street a block away. Hopefully, the flashy Lamborghini was still there and not drawing a ton of attention. "You'd have to take me into the city and it sounds like you have some sort of emergency."

"Yes."

That she didn't want to leave him in her apartment couldn't have been more obvious. He put a hand to his abdomen and tried to look harmless. "Go. I can wait for my friend outside. It won't take him more than forty-five minutes to get here."

Kelly frowned, obviously torn. The radio at her belt squawked to life. She reached for it and started briskly back down the hall toward her room. "Go ahead, Fred."

"Louis took a header off the second story of the Cook job. He's en route to the district hospital by ambulance right now. Looks like a concussion and a compound fracture of the leg. There could be other injuries. He landed on a pile of wood. It could be bad, Kelly."

"Tammy just called. You want me at the site or the hospital?"

"Hospital. I'll stay and handle the site."

"Okay. I'll let you know when I get there."

She returned a minute later, having donned a jean jacket over her blouse and holding a set of keys.

"I'm sorry, Mr. Maddox. I need to go right now. Just pull the front door closed tight when you leave. The bottom lock will engage."

"Thank you is inadequate."

"No, it isn't."

Her voice was firm. She'd been off balance since they'd met, but the emergency had returned her usual control in full measure.

"I'm glad I could help. Good luck. Oh, and would you find the cat and put her out before you leave?"

"Of course."

She was out the door before he could say more,

her concern for the injured worker palpable. Reece took his coffee to the dining-room table and pulled out his cell phone. The line rang a long time before a muzzy male voice answered.

"Do you know what bloody time it is?"

"Two-twelve," Reece told Heath Brockmorton. "I need your help."

"Reece? That you?"

"Yes. I'm stranded in suburbia without any clothes."

There was a beat of silence. "Is this a bloody joke?"

"Do you hear laughter?"

The line fell silent while Heath became more alert and processed the words. "This is a story I must hear."

"In person when you get here." By then Reece hoped he'd have a story ready.

"Where's here?"

Reece told him and added directions before hanging up. Heath had recently purchased a condo on the same floor as Reece's unit. Too bad they'd never exchanged keys in case of emergency.

He'd known Heath since college. They both came from wealth and moved in the same international circles. Despite his formal British upbringing, Heath was one of those laid-back guys who never seemed to take himself or anyone else too seriously. Reece liked him. And, more important to the current situation, the two of them wore exactly the same size.

He hadn't needed to call Heath, of course. He could have put on something belonging to Kelly's father. But Reece told himself he didn't want to draw attention by walking to his car in inexpensive, ill-fitting clothing. He didn't need to be stopped because someone thought he was stealing the Lamborghini. Also, Gene's clothes would stand out once he got to his building. There was a strong chance that a photographer or two might be hanging around his condo after last night's premiere, hoping to catch him with the leading lady. Reece could count on Heath's discretion, particularly if Reece told him a woman was involved.

Waiting in Gene's empty apartment felt strange. The two of them had always met at the trailer or a bar. Gene had lived in a furnished efficiency until he learned Kelly planned to come back to live with him until she got established. Reece missed his friend so much.

Idly, he skimmed through the papers on the table, relieved to see there was something addressed to Kelly, after all. He made sure that item was left on top to give credence to his earlier tale. Most of the papers were insurance forms and other matters pertaining to Gene's death, but Reece didn't let that stop him from skimming through them. Someone had wanted inside here last night and he needed to figure out why.

While the man could have been nothing more than a chance burglar, Reece hadn't stayed alive this long without trusting his instincts and his instincts were screaming. It was safer to assume his attacker had been the third person in the trailer that night. By using Gene and Curtis as couriers, Reece had made them targets and, by association, anyone connected with them. But, if the other side had the flash drive back as his agency had assumed, why was anyone interested in Kelly?

He used the time he had to go through the apartment as thoroughly as possible before the little gray cat appeared and stropped his leg. With a soft mew, it headed for the sliding-glass door where it paused to look back at him expectantly.

"Got the message, cat."

Reece let the animal out and stepped onto the small patio for a quick look around outside. The intruder had been picking the lock when Reece had interrupted, yet there wasn't a mark to show for the man's attempt. There was, however, a bloody knife, still lying in the grass halfway up the slope, that the cat had stopped to investigate. Quickly, Reece retrieved it. The blade was designed to fit in a sheath strapped to a leg.

He almost hoped his attacker was watching the apartment right now. Better to have the bastard coming after him than Kelly. If nothing else, last night had convinced Reece she wasn't safe here, but he'd need a solid ruse to get her to move somewhere else.

Back inside, he secured the lock and the useless bar with a scowl and picked up his cell phone. This number wasn't on speed dial.

"Finley's Laundry Service."

"I've got a pinstripe blue suit with a tear in it," he told the woman. "Do you do repairs?"

"Would you hold for a moment, please, sir?"

Not for the first time, Reece wondered if Finley's Laundry Service really did laundry. It probably did. Back when he'd first learned all these code words this had seemed like a game. What twenty-two-year-old didn't want to play secret agent for his country?

He was thirty-five now and the game was no longer fun. Mention of the pinstripe blue suit would get him transferred to another line. The reference to a tear told them he was calling from an unsecured line. Even now, they were, no doubt, running his cell-phone number to know exactly who he was and probably tracing the location he was calling from.

"How may I help you?" The new voice was masculine and one he recognized.

"I was at a party the other night and not only got a tear in my suit, but the hem is starting to unravel. I was wondering if you could mend this."

Translated, not only was he on an open line, but he was injured and his cover was in danger.

"You'll have to bring it by for us to look at, sir. Does it need repair immediately?"

"No," he wasn't in immediate danger—at least, he didn't think he was, "but it's my favorite suit." He would really like to know what was going on.

"If you can stop by around five, our seamstress will be available then, sir."

Reece glanced at his watch. Subtract two hours. He could possibly make it into D.C. by three-thirty if Heath got here in the next few minutes with some clothes, but he didn't dare leave Kelly without protection.

"I don't think I can make it there until five-thirty, will that be okay?"

"Yes, sir. Is there anything else?"

Reece hesitated. Kelly's safety wouldn't constitute an emergency in their eyes, but he had a lot of questions that required answers. Like why they were suppressing Arthur Weems's identification and whose operative had been sniffing around Kelly's home.

"No, thanks."

He disconnected and speed dialed a number. Caller ID would give Mark Ramsey his identity, so Reece didn't bother with preambles. "I need 24/7 coverage on her immediately."

"This have anything to do with this morning's events?"

Leave it to Mark to be on top of everything and cut right to the chase. Reece hadn't even considered the possibility that the accident at the construction site might have been a ruse to draw Kelly away from the apartment. He swore out loud.

"I'll take that as a yes. I'm on it."

"Hurry."

"You got it."

"Thanks."

"Wait until you see the bill."

Mark Ramsey was smart, discrete and good at what he did, which was specializing in private security. Reece knew just how private and how good since he'd bankrolled the start-up of Mark's firm several years ago. Mark was younger than Reece, but smart and ambitious. He'd paid back the loan with interest in less than three years. He hired good people who knew how to get a job done.

Reece had used Mark's people to install tight security in and around the warehouse he'd created after Kelly had insisted on continuing operations. For Mark, monitoring the warehouse around the clock was no problem. Ramsey Inc. operated from the group of warehouses one block down.

But, while accidents were an occupational hazard in construction, Mark's question had started Reece thinking. Someone wanted something from inside this apartment and it would be best if Reece found that something first.

Chapter Four

"You're killing me here, Kelly. You had Reece Maddox in your apartment last night? *Reece Maddox!*"

Beyond tired, Kelly shook her head at Leah and set the huge bouquet of flowers down on Tammy's desk before turning back to the lobby area.

"I know who he is, but I'm not sure the people in the warehouse behind this one heard you."

"Sorry, but he's gorgeous. And rich. Filthy rich!"

"And an international playboy, blah, blah, blah. Trust me, he bleeds red like the rest of us. There wasn't a trace of blue in his blood, I swear."

"I can't believe you. This was a once in a lifetime event and you left him sitting in your dad's apartment? How could you leave him sitting there?"

"Because Louis fell off a roof and broke his leg and fractured his arm and has a massive concussion and he works for me!"

"Well, for you and the vampire." Leah meant to let it drop but Kelly seized on it.

"He didn't show last night."

"What? Who? You mean, you did wait for the Midnight Prince again? I knew it! I told Jimmy that was why you wouldn't come with us."

Thankful to have diverted her friend, Kelly nodded. "I wasted a whole night sitting on the ground out back this time. He never showed. How could he have known I was there? I hid my car and everything. I swear, I'm going to search this place for bugs."

"What sort of—" Leah's eyes widened. "You think he has your office bugged?" Her voice dropped and she gazed around the reception area.

"Not really. I was kidding. Mostly."

"I don't know, Kelly. It would explain a lot, wouldn't it?"

Kelly pinched the bridge of her nose. "Do *not* go there."

"I'm just saying… At any rate, last night wasn't entirely a waste. If you hadn't gone home at four in the morning you'd never have met Reece Maddox."

"Great. Give me another reason to be depressed."

"Are you kidding? Look!"

She snatched up the newspaper someone had tossed on the couch and tore through it until she found the section she wanted.

"Here it is." She skimmed the article she'd

stopped at. "Are you sure it was him? Maybe it was just someone who looked like him."

"I'm sure."

"That's so weird. Reece Maddox was at the premiere for *Reelection* last night. You know, that hot new movie with Barcley Anderson."

"Who?"

Leah rolled her eyes. "Barcley Anderson. The new actress everyone is talking about. She's a native Washingtonian! I swear, Kelly you have got to stop living in this cave and get a life. See? There's a picture of the two of them right here next to the director and his wife."

"Let me see that."

The photo was grainy, but his features were indelibly stamped in her memory. Reece Maddox stood beside a phenomenally sleek woman dressed in a daringly sexy long gown. Another, less glamorous couple stood beside them. Reece and the other man both wore tuxedos.

Kelly sighed. "That's him."

"How can you act so blasé? Kelly, the man went from *her* to your apartment!"

"Hardly. And would you please keep your voice down to a low shout?"

"Who's going to hear? The rats?"

"We don't have rats."

"This is a warehouse surrounded by fields. Of course you have rats. Or mice."

"We do not have rodents."

"That's right, the vampire probably feeds on them so he won't turn to people."

"Leah!"

"Okay, so he has the place bugged. Who cares? I can't believe you just walked out and left Reece Maddox standing in your apartment! Injured, no less!"

"I didn't leave him standing there injured. Okay, I did, but I did what I could for his wounds last night."

"That is so romantic."

Kelly rolled her eyes. "There was nothing romantic about it. Would you be serious?"

"The man is knock-down gorgeous. You can't tell me you were immune. You had to be attracted to him!"

She would not think of him standing there in his briefs, lean and as beautifully sculpted as a living piece of art.

"Unless you're gay," Leah continued.

Exasperated, she glared at her friend. "I am not gay."

"So you did find him attractive!"

Kelly closed her eyes and counted a fast ten. "Leah, the man was hurt. I helped him the same way I would have helped anyone else. End of story."

"Reece Maddox is not just anyone. He's...Reece

Maddox! And you're just going to let him walk out of your life?"

Leah was not going to let it lie. She was working herself into a full-scale fantasy. Kelly shook her head.

"Of course not." She maintained a straight face. "I'm going to buy a rope and tie him to my father's bed so we can have wild monkey sex all night long."

Leah's eyes went wide. Her mouth gaped unbecomingly. Then she giggled. "Well, that's more like it."

"Will you quit? Leah, please. Promise me you'll keep this to yourself."

"Oh, no. Please don't ask me that. Can't I even tell Jimmy?"

"Absolutely not! Look, I can't afford the media to get hold of a story like this. Neither can he. That's why he asked me not to call the police."

"Hmm. I guess that's true enough."

"It is," Kelly stated firmly.

"But what was he doing there? Besides trying not to be robbed, I mean."

"Excellent question. I did ask, but we got… sidetracked."

"Please tell me it was by wild monkey sex."

"The man was injured! We did not have sex of any kind. Would you get your mind out of the sheets?"

"So you're going to just forget about him?"

Kelly's gaze fell on the picture once more. The grainy black-and-white photograph did not show the bright blue intensity of his intelligent eyes nor the subtle strength of the charisma that subverted good intentions and made a woman completely aware that he was fascinatingly male. Forget about him?

"If possible, that's exactly what I intend to do."

Leah regarded her with open skepticism. "I don't think he's going to let you."

"What are you talking about?"

"That!"

That was the enormous bouquet of flowers that had been delivered to Custom Concepts only minutes ago—unfortunately, in front of Leah. The card had fallen to the ground and Leah had picked it up. Immediately, she'd jumped to the wrong conclusion.

"Good grief. What did you do to earn *this* from the Midnight Prince?" she'd asked. *"Thank you for last night*? Kelly, you rat fink, you've been holding out on me. Is this a joke? It's signed Reece Maddox."

Now Kelly was deeply regretting the impulse that had made her confess what had really happened. On the other hand, with Leah holding the signed card, what was she supposed to do? She was far too drained to come up with a convincing story on the spur of the moment.

"He likes you," Leah insisted.

"Of course he does. I'm very likable. Leah, would you get serious. He's just grateful."

"As well he should be. Haven't you ever heard that patients fall in love with their nurses?"

Kelly rolled her eyes.

"This is the coolest thing that has ever happened to anyone I know," Leah continued. "You can't tell me I can't tell anyone. I'll burst at the seams."

"Sounds messy, but if you must, at least do it quietly." She rubbed her aching temples. "I've got the start of a humongous headache."

"Too much monkey sex. Want some aspirin? I have some in my purse."

"No. What I want is for you to go home so I can do the same. I need sleep, Leah. I'm going to have to come in tomorrow to fill out all the insurance claims on the accident."

"Tomorrow's Saturday."

"Which is just another day. I'm sure I'm going to be hearing from Mr. Prince about the accident and I want to be able to assure him I'm on top of things."

"You think he'll call you tonight?"

Kelly sighed. "Probably. Undoubtedly, if he gets my message."

"And he'll just expect you to be home, waiting for his call?" Leah shook her head. "You know what you need?"

"Please don't tell me."

"You need a man like Reece Maddox in your life."

"I asked you not to tell me."

"Someone tall, dark and handsome," Leah enthused, warming to her task. "Someone fabulously rich who will tell the vampire to get lost."

"Leah, go home." Kelly began backing her friend toward the front entrance. "Quitting time was over an hour ago. I'm sure you and Jimmy have plans for the evening."

"Not really. Kelly, you have to think of a way to stay in touch with him. You should go buy yourself a slinky dress and—"

"Go home." Kelly opened the door. "I am never going to see Reece Maddox again. I am going back to my father's quiet garden apartment where I am going to go to bed—alone!—and try to forget last night ever happened."

"But a chance like this only happens once in a lifetime. You can't throw this opportunity away."

"Watch me." She gave her friend a gentle shove. "I'll see you on Monday."

"But I thought you might want to come over… Oh." She breathed as her eyes widened.

Kelly followed her friend's glassy eyed stare as an expensive-looking shiny black convertible sports car pulled into the parking space directly in front of them. She forgot to breathe. The car was sleek and dangerous-looking but that was nothing compared with the man dressed in black who stepped out of the door that slid up and forward like the raised wing of some evil dark bird.

Reece Maddox strolled toward her, all supple, masculine grace, as if it was the most natural thing in the world for him to do.

Kelly put a hand to her temple. "I'll take that aspirin now."

She did not want this sudden rush of unwanted anticipation zinging through her. There was only the slightest hitch in his carriage to remind her that he'd been injured. She exhaled sharply.

"What are you *doing* here? How did you even know where here *is?*"

Reece removed the band of dark sunglasses that covered his eyes. "We have a problem."

"Yes! You. Here," she managed. And then reason kicked in with a jolt of fear. "Are you okay? What's wrong?"

He looked all right. He looked better than all right. Standing there in the approaching dusk, he looked downright devastating.

"I'm fine, Kelly. Thanks to you."

He was fine. Then, why was he here? How dare he smile that innocent, killer smile at her? He was standing here where anyone might see him and call the press.

"You certainly are," Leah breathed.

"Aren't you going to introduce me to your friend?" he asked.

"No!"

"I'm Leah," she told him stepping forward. "Leah Wickliff. Don't mind Kelly, she has a headache."

"You do?" He looked to her again, all concern in those deep blue eyes.

"Yes." And her headache was standing right in front of her, all six feet plus inches of him.

"I'm Reece Maddox, Leah."

"Oh, I know who you are," she agreed in a rush. "Kelly told me all about last night."

"Really? Everything?" His eyebrows arched suggestively.

Leah's eyes widened. "What everything? There was an everything?"

"No! There was not an everything! I told you what happened." She rounded on him. "Will you stop that?"

Reece spread his hands in innocence. "*I* didn't tell anyone about last night."

"I knew it!" Leah exclaimed. "You left out the good parts!"

"There were no good parts!"

"I could remedy that," he offered, his expression teasing while Leah practically drooled.

"Stop it! Why did you sign the card with your name?"

"Ah, the flowers. I'm glad you got them. Did you want me to make a name up so you wouldn't know who sent them to you? I didn't want one of your boyfriends to take the credit."

"She doesn't have any boyfriends," Leah told him.

"I don't believe that for a minute."

Kelly spared a glare for her friend and rounded on him. "I told you thanks was enough."

"Hardly. She saved my life," he told Leah.

"I did no such thing. You weren't in danger of dying from a couple of minor cuts."

"You're the one who told me they needed stitches."

"That's 'cause she's into bondage," Leah inserted.

"Leah!" Horrified, she gaped at her friend.

Reece raised his eyebrows in question.

"Kelly's planning to tie you to her father's bed and have wild monkey sex with you."

"You're a dead woman."

"Wild monkey sex?" His tone was mild, but humor danced in his voice and the eyes he deliberately didn't turn toward her. "Sounds primitive."

"It does, doesn't it? Now that I've seen you up close I can appreciate the feeling. Jimmy always said the right man would melt her inhibitions and turn her into a wild woman."

"D-E-A-D," Kelly promised.

"See?"

"Leah, go home. Why are you *here*?" she demanded of Reece.

· "I told you, we have a problem."

Her stomach fluttered like a wild thing. "What sort of a problem?"

"Do you want to stand out here and talk about it or could we go inside?"

"I don't want to talk about anything with you. I want to go home and sleep the clock around, but that isn't going to happen, is it?"

"Afraid not." His expression became contrite. "You can't go home. Your home is under siege at the moment."

"What?" she and Leah chorused.

"Let's go inside and I'll explain. We probably don't have much time."

"Much time for what?" But she allowed him to herd them back inside the warehouse. Kelly turned to Leah as they entered the waiting room. "Don't you have someplace to be?"

"Not a chance!"

"Isn't Jimmy waiting for you?"

"Jimmy who?"

Kelly sighed and pinched the bridge of her nose.

"You really do have a headache." Reece oozed concerned sympathy.

"Yes. What do you mean, the apartment is under

siege? What sort of siege?" Kelly demanded, even though she knew with that sinking feeling of dread exactly what he was talking about.

"Someone alerted the media I was there. They took a picture of me coming out carrying my old clothing."

"Oh, God. Did they see the blood?"

"No. But I'm afraid they think we're having an affair."

Kelly gaped at him.

"Oh, wow." Leah's eyes grew enormous. "They'll be all over her."

"Afraid so," Reece agreed. "I saw this company listed on some of the papers on your table. I wasn't prying, Kelly, they were sitting out in plain sight. I put that together with your emergency call this afternoon and figured I'd come here and warn you."

"What were you doing near her apartment in the first place?" Leah asked.

Kelly stiffened alertly.

"That is a rather long, embarrassing story and I'm not sure we have time to go into it at the moment."

"Make time," Kelly demanded.

He cocked his head at her. "If I can track you here, so can the media."

"Remind me to kill that cat," Kelly muttered.

"What cat? You didn't say anything about a cat,"

Leah protested. "Only monkeys. Does the cat go with the monkeys?"

Reece cupped Kelly's arm. Even through the denim of her jacket she felt the power of that touch.

"I assure you, Kelly, this will all blow over in a few days. A week, at most."

"A week? I don't have a week. I have a company to run."

"Surely, you don't run it all by yourself."

"No," Leah cut in, "her partner's an invisible vampire."

"Leah!"

"What?" he asked at the same time, obviously startled.

"Never mind. I need to think." Kelly pinched the bridge of her nose again.

"Maybe we should do that somewhere else. Have you eaten?"

She stared at him, trying to process the words. Her brain was spinning at the nightmare consequences this would have. She wanted the police to take her seriously, not view her as some sort of groupie.

"I doubt it," Leah answered for her. "Birds eat more than she does. That's probably why she has a headache."

He nodded. "Leah, the press will be all over everyone for a few days. I'd take it as a personal favor if you wouldn't say anything to anyone about what happened today."

"I'm not even sure what *did* happen."

Kelly closed her eyes.

"But I won't say anything. Kelly's my friend."

"Thank you. She's my friend, too. I take it this is a construction company. What do you build?"

"Houses," Leah told him.

"Perfect. If anyone asks, you can tell them I came to talk to her company about building a house for me."

Kelly glared at him. "And you were coming out of my apartment with a change of clothing be-cause…why?"

"We'll work on that over dinner."

"I can't go to dinner with you!"

"Why not? We both have to eat and Leah says you aren't troubled by a pesky boyfriend."

"Leah is so dead."

Reece smiled. "Don't worry about the paparazzi. I know the perfect place to take you."

"I'll bet you do," Leah agreed dreamily.

He flashed her a smile and turned back to Kelly. "We can work on a convincing story to spin. Actually, I have been thinking about buying a house and settling down. This is the perfect out for both of us. Please, Kelly. I owe you dinner, at the very least."

"He does," Leah agreed. "You should go. The man drives a Lamborghini."

"A what?"

"And we need to talk about where you're going to spend the night," Reece added in a slow, sexy drawl.

Leah's mouth gaped open again while a tingle of sensual awareness woke a womanly response Kelly hadn't felt in along time. She did not want to be attracted to this man. She was trying very hard not to think about him in that way.

Trying, but failing miserably.

"I'm not interested in being the newest notch on your bed post." She regretted the words as soon as they tumbled past her lips.

His intense blue eyes yielded to something she couldn't decipher.

"My bed doesn't have posts, notched or unnotched," he told her with deceptive mildness. "And you really should wait to be asked, don't you think?"

"Sorry. I shouldn't have said that."

"No, you shouldn't have. If you don't want to have dinner with me, say so, Kelly."

Of course she didn't. And she squashed down the tiny voice inside that called her a liar. He was too suave, too handsome, too rich and definitely too dangerous for her peace of mind. Besides, she was too tired. But what choice was there?

"Let me check the back door and grab my purse. We do need to talk."

She didn't look at Leah as she hurried down the hall, but she cringed as she heard her friend begin talking again earnestly. Who knew what would spill past Leah's lips without someone there to muzzle her?

The back door was locked and bolted as always, papers neatly arranged on the desk waiting for the mysterious James Prince's attention. Funny how fast priorities could change. If he walked in the door right this minute it would be anticlimactic after the day she'd had.

She turned out the light, strode into her office and lifted her purse, pausing for a moment to stare at the pictures of her father.

"Wish you were here, Dad. I could really use some advice about now. I'm in over my head and too tired to think straight," she whispered. For a long moment, she closed her eyes and just stood there. "Miss you, Dad."

Turning off the light, she headed down the hall to where Reece Maddox waited. Alone.

"Where's Leah?"

"She had to go meet…Jimmy, was it?"

"Her boyfriend."

"Yes. Are you all right?"

"Super."

"You're good at sarcasm. Just the right curl to your tone."

"It's been a long day."

"I know the feeling. Come on, my car's right outside."

She hesitated, doing her best to ignore the zing of attraction that was making her words sound sharper than usual. "So is my truck." Her father's truck, actually, but now hers. She'd taken the truck after Fred Vargas had called, leaving her car at the apartment.

"I'll bring you back for it later."

"I'd rather drive myself."

He had an unnerving way of looking at her, as if he could see right through her to the real reason she was reluctant to get in the car with him.

"Had much experience outrunning photographers?"

That brought her up short. "There are photographers out there?"

"I don't know, but there could be by now. Shall we go find out?" He opened the front door.

"Remind me never to feed another stray animal as long as I live."

The corners of his mouth twisted up in the start of another smile and she turned her back to set the dead bolt. He was standing too close. Close enough for her to pick up that familiar, pleasing, light masculine scent she'd noticed before. Close enough that it took her three tries to fit the key in the lock. She turned it at last and looked up at him. He smiled. A camera flash went off practically in her eyes.

Chapter Five

"Mr. Maddox! Look this way!"

"Come on." Reece caught Kelly's arm and propelled her to the passenger door of his sleek black sports car. She had a fleeting moment to question why it didn't open outward like any normal, self-respecting car door and then she was inside as more photographs were taken.

The man called to him again as a second car pulled up. Kelly closed her eyes. Reece slid behind the wheel, started the engine and roared out of the parking space.

"Seat belt," he ordered harshly.

Kelly found the belt and put it on. She needed it, because they were going to be killed. The idiot was driving like this was a raceway. "Slow down!"

"In a minute."

They tore out of the parking lot, whipped down the deserted side street, peeled around a corner and slid through a yellow traffic light. Half a block later, he turned right onto the main thoroughfare. In a matter of minutes they were on the highway, knifing through Friday-night traffic as if it wasn't there.

"If we don't die, I'm going to kill you."

He flashed her that famous boyish grin. "Relax. I think we lost them."

"And my lunch, if I'd eaten any lunch today."

"Sorry."

"I can tell." They were heading north with traffic, rather than south toward D.C. She had to shout over the sound of the wind and cars. "Where are we going?"

"A little place I know. Anonymity guaranteed."

"Right. You planning to turn invisible? Maybe change this status symbol into a minivan?"

The grin returned. "Trust me."

"You wish."

"You wound me."

"No, I leave that to guys with knives. I've got no interest in your wallet."

"That alone makes you a refreshing change."

Kelly thought about that for a second and decided sadly it was probably true. People such as Reece Maddox were always pursued by those who wanted what his wealth and fame could buy. She fell silent as he maneuvered the car with a deft ease she had to admire, even as her breath caught and she tensed over a few close calls.

"Wherever we're going better not be fancy. I am not dressed for fancy."

"You're fine. Perfect."

"Uh-huh." She lapsed into silence rather than continue to yell over the rush of air.

Having never ridden in a convertible, let alone an exotic sports car before, she was surprised to discover how exciting it could be. The little car hugged the ground close enough to feel every little dip and rise in the surface of the road. Dwarfed by everything else around them, the car made it easy to dart into the smallest opening and pass the other vehicles with incredible ease.

The pins and scrunchy holding up her hair didn't have a chance. Kelly freed them and caught Reece's smile of approval as strands of hair whipped about in a ribbon of red tangles. She found herself smiling back while she tried to keep her hair from whipping into her eyes.

All too soon the headlong ride was over. Reece got off the highway and, after a stretch, pulled into a long, open dirt driveway that led to a sprawling stone house. The front of if it had been built around the time of the Civil War, but generations had added to the structure over the years.

"Where are we?"

"Haverdock Inn. It's a bed-and-breakfast as well as a good place to eat. I know the owners."

"You're full of surprises, aren't you?"

"I try."

Reece bypassed the parking lot and drove around to the back of the building. This part could prove to be a little tricky, but he hoped he could head off trouble before it happened.

From the rear the major additions were easy to distinguish. What was now the main dining room overlooked a large stone patio with a great view of the duck pond and the mountains in the distance. Reece walked around to the passenger side of the car and opened the door for Kelly before she could open it herself. He thought she might ignore his hand, but she wasn't used to climbing out of such a low-slung vehicle and her hand slipped into his.

"Thank you."

The blue of her eyes still sparkled from the ride and she pushed uselessly at her tangled hair. He thought she'd never looked prettier.

Her hand was small and delicate in his, but the skin wasn't butter soft and pampered like the women's he was used to escorting. Kelly's nails were cropped short and neatly trimmed as befitted someone who was used to working with her hands. Her grip was firm and he found himself smiling back at her in genuine pleasure.

"So what did you think?"

She didn't play coy. "That was fun. Scary, but fun. You're an amazing driver."

"Thank you. Training and years of practice. There was a time in my misspent youth that I wanted to be a race-car driver." He took her elbow and guided her to the back door.

"What happened?"

"I grew up."

She smiled back at him. "Ah, isn't this the kitchen entrance?"

"You want to go unnoticed, don't you?"

"Yes, and I'm sure that no one in the kitchen of a busy restaurant will notice a couple of guests sneaking inside."

He chuckled and squeezed her fingers lightly. "Trust me."

Before they reached the door it swung open and Mary stood there beaming. "Mr—"

"Just Reece, Mary," he got in quickly. "How are you?"

She didn't so much as blink an eye at the change in name. He generally used James Prince when he came here for dinner. "Wonderful, Reece. It's so good to see you again."

"Can you fit us in somewhere quiet, Mary?"

"Of course. The small, private room isn't reserved tonight. Do you also want a room for the night?"

Kelly shook her head quickly. "No."

"Yes," he said at the same time.

Mary smiled serenely. "I'll let the two of you work that one out. I'll have a room available if you decide you want it."

"We won't," Kelly assured her, face bright pink.

Reece gave Mary a slight nod and she turned, ushering them through the busy kitchen. There was a sharp jab in his side as Kelly elbowed him hard. Fortunately, it wasn't his injured side.

The busy staff barely spared them a glance. Mary led them down a side hall to a room that could easily seat twenty and had a terrific view of the pond and the scenery beyond.

"Lisa will be right with you."

"Thanks, Mary. Be sure to tell Allan to pop in and say hello."

"I'll do that. Enjoy your meal." And she disappeared, closing the door in her wake.

Kelly gazed around the peacefully understated surroundings. "We're going to have this entire room to ourselves?"

"Anonymity. I told you." He pulled off his sunglasses and smiled at her.

"Right. Mary knows who you are."

"And doesn't care."

"I can see where that would be a plus for someone like you."

He cocked his head, not sure he liked the *someone like you* reference.

"I'd hate to be a celebrity," she added.

Reece relaxed. "It has its moments."

"Uh-huh. How are you feeling? Really."

There was genuine concern in her gaze and he found himself telling her the truth.

"Frankly, the cuts hurt more than I expected."

"You should be resting, not running around all over the place. Did you have a doctor look at them?"

"I did." The enigmatic Mr. Smith had arranged for one. "He said you did a good job. However, you were right about a probable scar."

"I did warn you."

He smiled. "You did."

The door opened and a waitress appeared along with a busboy. The latter cleared extra plates and glasses from a linen covered table near the window. They took seats and waited in silence as he filled their water goblets and lit a small candle.

The woman produced menus and a wine list.

"Do you prefer red or white?" he asked Kelly.

"I've never cared much for wine. Too sour."

"Trust me?"

"To do what?"

He grinned. "To order for us, for starters."

"That depends. You aren't into funky stuff like snails and toad livers are you?"

"Toad livers?"

Kelly shrugged.

"I promise, no toad livers. Pipe up if I order something you don't like."

"Okay. It's your dollar." She sat back and stared out the bank of windows overlooking the darkening landscape while he ordered. Lisa was an experienced waitress, quiet and efficient and not, thank God, awed by his presence. She listened, repeated the order back, looked to Kelly for confirmation and disappeared at her nod.

Reece studied Kelly. Tension gathered in the set of her posture, but that was to be expected. She was handling the situation far better than he had any right to expect, but he didn't fool himself, she was near the end of her tolerance and he was about to give it another push.

"I think you should take a room here tonight."

"Why doesn't that surprise me?"

She didn't even turn to look at him. Not a good sign. "I said *you* should take a room."

She looked at him then. "There's nothing wrong with my hearing. Nor is there anything wrong with the perfectly good room I already have at my dad's apartment."

"It's being staked out by paparazzi."

"So you say."

"It's the truth, Kelly." And she'd be furious if she

learned he'd arranged for that to happen. Alerting the media was the quickest thing he could think of to keep her from going back there again until he figured out what was going on.

For an uncomfortably long moment, she gazed at him without speaking. "I've been a pretty good sport about all this, wouldn't you say?"

"You've been terrific."

She nodded. "Then, what were you doing outside my apartment last night?"

Reece hadn't come up with a suitable explanation. He didn't think she'd buy into car trouble considering how far off the main thoroughfare the apartment was located. And, looking into her eyes, he realized he didn't want to tell her any more lies.

"I'd really rather not say."

Her eyes narrowed. After a long moment of silence, she sat back. Her fingers tapped the edge of the table. "Fine. How long will they stay? The press," she clarified. "How long before the furor dies down?"

"A few days."

"Two? Three? More?"

She was angry and growing more so by the second. "I can't give you a timetable, Kelly."

"What can you give me, Reece?"

"Protection."

Her head swung from side to side sending reflected light dancing amid the tangled strands of golden-red hair.

"I've been fending for myself a long time now. You'd be surprised how good I am at it."

He expelled a sigh. "You've never faced hungry paparazzi before. Unfortunately, stories about me are part of their bread and butter. They're going to do their best to turn this into a front-page tabloid story."

"You may be as wealthy as a prince, but Cinderella's hugely overdone," Kelly scoffed, "and I don't fancy playing beast to your beauty."

His lips curved. "That could never happen. So build me a house."

"What?"

"Seriously. Let's give them something dull to gnaw on. You build houses. Build one for me."

"Just like that."

"If it's just business between us, there's no story."

Lisa returned with a bottle of champagne and began to open it.

"What's this?" Kelly asked.

"You said wine tastes sour. I promise you, this won't."

Her lips parted as he and Lisa went through the ritual of sniffing and tasting before the waitress discretely withdrew along with the busboy that had come in on her heels to set a basket of fresh baked rolls and pats of softened butter on the table.

"This isn't a date, Reece."

"No," he agreed, "it's dinner. I'm serious about the house, Kelly." He sipped at the champagne as she considered that.

"Would you have come to me to build you one if it hadn't been for last night?"

"Honestly? No. I'd have called a realtor and wasted days looking at places that didn't suit. This way I get exactly what I want, where I want."

"And you want what? Exactly."

You. With unsettling clarity he knew it was true. He knew so much about Gene's little girl, but now he was determined to learn about the woman she'd become. Reece wanted to know more. A lot more.

"I want you to build me a house, Kelly. Nothing pretentious, I'm talking a place to live with enough land not to feel closed in. I'm working on getting a pilot's license right now so it would be nice to have room for a small airstrip or to locate near an existing one. Water would be nice, a pond or stream or something, but not essential."

"You're serious."

He heard his enthusiasm growing and it surprised him to realize that he did want these things. "I am, yes."

"What sort of a house?" she asked cautiously.

"I don't know. Something sprawling, you know, spread out with plenty of room."

"For entertaining?"

"I was thinking more along the lines of a family."

Surprise was replaced by a flicker of skepticism she made no effort to conceal. Reece smiled. "Being a playboy gets old after a while."

"Okay. Where do you want this house? Custom Concepts is only licensed in Maryland, Virginia and D.C."

"Maryland, I think. My family lives in Virginia. A little distance is a good thing where family is concerned, especially mine. There's still some land right around here." He gestured to include the inn.

"And it costs top dollar," she warned.

He smiled more easily. "I can afford top dollar."

"I guess you can."

"Is my money a problem, Kelly?"

"For the sort of place you're talking about I'd say it's vital. I'm sure my partner will be thrilled over a coup like this. You'll put us on the map."

His stomach gave a funny little twist. "Your partner."

"James Prince," she agreed with a nod.

This was going to get complicated. "What's he like?"

"Elusive."

Reece tried not to smile. "That's a strange adjective to use about a partner."

"You have no idea."

"What's that supposed to mean?"

"Never mind."

He couldn't suppress the urge to tease her just a little. "I suppose I'll need to meet with him. Your partner will probably want to wine and dine me."

"No. He's...I guess you'd call him a silent partner. Custom Concepts is an investment for him. I handle the business end of things."

"Really?"

Her eyes narrowed. "Do you have a problem working with a woman?"

"On the contrary, I enjoy working with women." He offered her a slow smile. It was wrong to provoke her, but Gene had always said she needed to lighten up. Kelly had a tendency to take everything seriously.

"I thought you told me not to believe everything I read."

"Ouch. Guess I deserved that."

"Guess you did."

He smiled then, a genuine smile of pleasure. Kelly could hold her own. She wasn't impressed with him or his money and he found himself badly wanting her to be comfortable around him.

"So you'll do it? You'll build me a house?"

She hesitated. He lifted his glass, held it out toward her and waited. After a moment, she lifted hers, as well. They clinked together gently.

"To our partnership."

"To your house," she corrected, and took a tentative sip. Her eyes widened. "This is good."

"Glad you approve. Now, about this house…I'm thinking we should look for an old farmhouse, tear it down and start from scratch."

As night settled beyond the windows, he began to elaborate on plans he hadn't realized he'd consciously formed. Over the leisurely dinner, she asked questions, pointed out flaws and made suggestions. In turn, he regaled her with stories of people and types of architecture in places he had stayed. He watched as her clever mind began tumbling with ideas and sparks of genuine excitement over the possibilities.

Kelly could barely restrain her enthusiasm when she finally realized Reece was serious. The sort of place he wanted would be worth big money. She might even make enough of a profit to buy James Prince out years before she'd expected. Assuming, of course, he would actually let her buy him out when the time came. But she'd worry about James Prince later. This truly was a once in a lifetime chance and she wasn't about to blow it.

As she finished the last bite of a sinfully delicious tart, Reece reached for the champagne bottle once more and she covered her glass with her hand. "Enough."

It dawned on her that he'd been keeping her glass full while he was still nursing his initial glass. No wonder she was starting to feel warm and relaxed. She'd drunk most of a bottle of champagne by herself.

"Are you trying to get me drunk?"

"Absolutely not. Are you feeling drunk?"

Was she? She'd eaten a lot of food with the champagne. "Well, I'm not feeling entirely sober."

"Then you should stop. Drink your coffee."

Kelly reached for her cup. The coffee, like everything else tonight, was truly excellent. "You aren't what I expected."

"What did you expect?"

Not someone she could like. Not someone funny and intelligent and down-to-earth and really interesting. She hadn't, for a minute, forgotten how devastatingly attractive he was. Impossible, with him sitting across from her and the soft light playing over those handsome features. No wonder the media liked to take his picture so often. No doubt a face like his sold a lot of papers.

"Kelly?"

"Sorry. Guess I drifted off for minute there."

"I'm aware of my reputation, but it's highly exaggerated. I don't bed every woman I'm attracted to any more than you sleep with every man who asks you."

She cursed her fair complexion, knowing her cheeks were growing pink once more.

"That said," he continued, "I hope you'll take this the way it's meant. I think it would be best if you'd take the room here for tonight at my expense."

She set down her cup. He held up his hand to stave off the protest she hadn't begun to formulate.

"The press will be hanging around, Kelly. They won't give you a moment's peace if I take you home. I feel responsible for the position I've put you in."

"You *are* responsible!"

"Exactly. That's why I'm suggesting you take a room here tonight. Maybe for the next couple of days. In the morning, I'll have my spokesperson explain the situation to the media and we'll wait for the hype to die down."

She should not have drunk so much champagne. "You make it all sound so reasonable."

"It is reasonable."

Was it? "Even if I wanted to spend the night here, I don't have anything with me."

He smiled and she ordered her hormones to stand down.

"I believe I mentioned there are advantages to being me. Having money makes things happen."

"Like what?"

"Give me a few minutes. By the time you go upstairs, you'll have everything you need. I'll be right back."

"Hold it! I didn't agree to anything," she objected as he rose to his feet.

"I know. I just need to use the restroom."

"Oh." She watched him stride from the room, cheeks hot. Actually, all of her was hot. She had to keep in mind that most women reacted to Reece Maddox that way.

But he was more than just a sexy man. They didn't have a single thing in common, but she liked him. A lot. More than was probably good for her.

Somehow he'd disarmed her completely. She wasn't drunk, but she was more relaxed than she'd been since her father's murder. Ignoring the pinch of guilt accompanying that thought, she decided to seek out the ladies' room before Reece came back. She needed to think. Splashing cold water on her face might help.

Their waitress pointed her in the right direction and the water did help, but the mirror showed her what a wreck her hair was. As she went searching through her purse for her comb, she noticed her cell phone blinking. Leah had called, not once, but several times.

Kelly did what she could to tame her hair first, though it was pretty much beyond a mere comb's efforts. Then she took an extra minute to call her friend back. Leah answered on the first ring.

"Kelly! Where are you?" her friend demanded. "Are you all right?"

"Of course I'm all right. What's wrong?"

"Are you with Reece?"

"Yes. We just finished dinner."

"Wow. Never mind. Tell me all the details later. You shouldn't go home right now. Jimmy and I turned on the ten o'clock news a few minutes ago and they're showing pictures of you and Reece Maddox. They're calling you his new girlfriend."

It was after ten? Kelly couldn't believe they'd been sitting there in that empty room talking all this time. Where had the evening gone?

"Must be a slow news night."

"No, you don't understand. Someone killed a man outside your apartment tonight!"

Chapter Six

"What?" Kelly clenched her cell phone more tightly.

"A freelance photographer was waiting for you to get home near the tree line above your apartment. His partner was in the parking lot out front. The partner told the police they expected Reece to bring you home and they were there to take pictures of the two of you. A man out walking his dog found the dead guy and called the police. Whoever killed him stole his camera. Kelly, the man's neck was broken!"

For a stunned moment Kelly could only stand there staring at her shocked reflection. She kept seeing Reece trying to get to his feet after being knifed last night by those same trees. This couldn't be coincidence even if the cameraman hadn't been knifed. Was it possible her father's murderer was coming after her? She'd been raising such a fuss with people that maybe he felt she was a threat.

"Kelly? Are you there?"

She struggled to control her heaving stomach as it threatened to disgorge everything she'd just eaten. "I'm here."

"Don't go home, Kelly. Police and news crews are all over your building. You can spend the night here with me."

And put Leah at risk, too? Kelly didn't think so. "Thanks, but I have a place to stay. I'll call you back tomorrow. Thanks, Leah."

Kelly hung up before her friend could protest further. Her hand was shaking when she shoved the phone back in her purse. Numb with shock, she stepped out into the hall. Reece was waiting for her there.

"I just talked to Leah. She said—"

"I know. Not here. Come on." He took her arm. Instead of returning to the dining room, he led her up a flight of back stairs to a spacious corner bedroom over the dining area where they'd eaten dinner.

"What are you doing?"

"Allan told me what happened. He's going to bring us up a television set," he told her.

"You have to go to the police, Reece. You have to tell them what happened last night."

Reece looked grim. "Let's see what they say on television first."

They waited in silence for the start of the eleven o'clock news. A still shot of the two of them outside her office and one of them driving away accompanied images of the police cordon and excited neighbors looking on outside the apartment building. The report itself was, as usual, sketchy on details and big on interviews with neighbors.

"We need to go," she told him.

"And do what? Stand around with your other neighbors and stare at the remains?"

Kelly gaped at the harsh words. He immediately softened his tone. "There's nothing either of us can do at the moment."

"You can tell them what happened to you! It can't be a coincidence that you and the dead man were both attacked outside my apartment. My father's killer doesn't care who he hurts."

Reece almost pointed out that if a killer was coming after her he was certainly drawing a lot of attention to himself when he realized that Reece Maddox wouldn't know anything about her father or his death.

"Your father was killed outside your apartment, too?"

"No! Oh, you don't know about my father."

"Maybe you'd better tell me."

Guilt rode him hard as he listened.

"The police insist it was a drunken brawl, but too many things don't add up," she concluded. "For one, they've never identified the second body found with his. They say he was probably a drifter. And they expect me to believe my father sat there having a drink with the man. The police and their conjectures don't fit my father. I've called every person Dad ever knew, asking for help." Kelly's hands clenched and unclenched at her sides. "I don't know what else to do, but there's more to what happened and I'm not giving up until I learn what it is. That's why we need to talk to the police. What if there was a third person in the trailer that night?"

Mentally, he winced. "What if there was? Why would he be trying to kill strangers outside your apartment?"

"I don't know," she admitted wearily.

"Kelly, I'm not saying you're wrong. And we will talk to the police, but not tonight. We're both tired."

"Not that tired."

"I am. And this won't be a matter of simply talking to the police. The media is going to start hounding us the moment they know where we are. It's what they do, Kelly."

"Let them. I can't just go to sleep like nothing's happened."

"I know." He took her clenched fist and the fingers uncurled. "We'll talk to the police, but we'll do it on our terms. Our information won't help them solve this murder tonight. You know that." He gentled his tone. "You've never been caught in a media circus before. It's ugly, Kelly."

"Uglier than a man with his neck broken?" She drew in a ragged breath. "Sorry."

"Like I said, we're both tired. We need some rest before we talk to the police."

A discrete tap at the door interrupted them. Mary stood in the hall holding a shopping bag with the items he'd asked her for. "Here you go, Reece."

"Thanks, Mary. I'll talk with you in a few minutes." He closed the door before Kelly reached them. "What is that?"

"Nightgown, toothbrush, other toiletries."

"I hope the nightgown is your color," she snapped at him. "I didn't agree to stay here tonight."

"I know. I asked Mary to pull together a few things for you when I heard what had happened. I can't stop you if you're determined to leave, but I'm not going with you. I'll have Allan call a cab. You might want to bear in mind that the detectives assigned to this case will be busy processing the scene. It's unlikely they'll get around to talking with you for hours. And the truth is, we have no information that will aim them at a particular suspect or even convince them the cases are connected."

Her shoulders sagged. Reece lightly rubbed his thumb over the back of her hand. "Stay here tonight. Rest if you can't sleep. Tomorrow will be soon enough to talk to the authorities."

She withdrew her hand self-consciously. Reece had

known more beautiful women, but none more compelling. Her beauty was inside and out. Kelly gave her all to the things and people she cared about. She had strong principles and an innate sense of kindness.

She'd had so much to deal with, and all of it was his fault. In order to mitigate the situation, there were people he needed to talk with tonight and they didn't include the police.

"It just feels wrong not to be doing something." She didn't look at him. Her gaze wandered to the bag he'd set on the floor.

"I know. Get some rest, Kelly." He reached for the door handle.

"Where are you going?"

"I need to make a couple of phone calls."

"I meant…" She cleared her throat. "Where are you going to sleep?"

"I'll see if Mary has another room."

"And, if she doesn't?"

He smiled gently. "Are you offering to share?"

"No!" She winced and color pinked her face once more. "Sorry. I didn't mean to sound so…so…."

"Horrified?"

She glared at him. His lips stayed curved. "You have to admit my ego's taking a terrible beating with you."

"Your ego will survive just fine."

"Hey, I'm a sensitive guy."

"Uh-huh." A flash of sudden panic had her grabbing for his arm again. "Reece, did you let the cat out before you left today? I don't have a litter box and I didn't leave her much food. All the commotion outside will scare her."

Relieved her panic was only due to the cat, he touched her cheek lightly, saw the flare of awareness in the depths of her eyes and felt her quiver at his touch. Oddly satisfying, even if the timing couldn't have been worse.

"I let her out. I'm sure the cat's fine."

She let go of his arm and took a step back, almost tripping on the bag he'd set on the floor.

"You're probably right. It's just that she's a timid little thing."

"Really? That's not the impression I got."

"I've been wooing her."

"Lucky cat."

Her gaze flashed to his, a mix of desire, panic and uncertainty. He wanted to kiss those soft lips. He wanted to run his hands through that silken mass of red hair. She took another step back as if sensing his thoughts and lifted the bag Mary had given him.

"You'd better go see about a room before they're all gone."

He hesitated a second because he still wanted to kiss her, then reached for the door handle again.

"You'll let me know?" she asked. "If there's a room for you? You won't just leave?"

"I won't just leave. I'll be back after I talk with the Haverdocks."

"Okay."

Reece stepped into the hall and tried to stop thinking about her lips as he pulled out his cell phone and crossed to the back staircase. There was no one around so he paused on the landing to call Mark Ramsey.

"You and Kelly okay?" Mark asked as soon as he picked up.

"Fine. I gather you heard what happened. You've got our location?"

"Only because of the transponder we attached to your car. Nice driving, by the way. You didn't ask me to cover her place." He sounded annoyed at that last bit.

"I know. My mistake. Send someone over to see if they can find a small gray cat hanging around the scene."

"I didn't know she had a pet."

"It's a stray Kelly's been feeding."

"Any markings?"

He thought back. "White under the chin and three white paws."

"Okay. I've got someone there, already, but it'll cost you extra if my operative gets scratched."

Reece grinned. "Deal. Any info yet the police didn't release to the media?"

"Depends. Does your girlfriend make a habit of leaving her sliding-glass door unlocked?"

His stomach churned. "I locked it before I left." So the guy had come back. If Kelly hadn't been with him it could have been her body the police were processing. The thought was intolerable. It was bad enough that he was going to have to live with the death of Kelly's father and now the photographer on his conscience, but he wasn't sure how he'd cope if it had been Kelly.

"The photographer must have taken the guy's picture," he muttered out loud, "probably when he left the apartment." A guess, but it felt right.

"That's the way I have it figured, too," Mark agreed. "Want to bet the cops are of the same mind?"

"They know someone was inside?"

"The guy tossed the place and he wasn't worried about finesse. One of the cops noticed the mess through the window. I guess they found the door unlocked. Either he was sloppy or he didn't care and I'm going for the latter, because this guy killed like a pro. No hesitation, no signs of a struggle. I'd say he spotted the cameraman, suspected the guy took his picture, made like he was walking off, then doubled back and snuck up behind the guy. The authorities are going to want to talk with the two of you."

Reece ran a hand through his hair. "Ray Hubbard's my next call."

"Lawyers do have their uses," Mark agreed. "I have an operative across the street from your location. You want her to come inside?"

"No, but tell her to stay sharp. I don't think anyone could have followed us here."

"They couldn't," he agreed.

"Assuming the killer didn't find what he's looking for, he'll try the warehouse next."

"Covered."

Of course it was. "The incident this morning?"

"No sign that it was anything other than an accident."

"What do you know that hasn't been released about the death of Kelly's father?"

Mark didn't miss a beat. "The top cops aren't happy. Someone with bigger badges stepped in and sealed the scene. The locals were given a simple explanation and told to make it stick. You know anything about that?"

"More than I want and not nearly enough." Reece had always suspected Mark knew of his connection to the agency, but the man was smart enough not to ask.

"Brilliantly evasive."

"I need to talk to some people."

"Think it will do you any good?"

"You're too young to be so cynical, Mark." But Mark was right. The agency wasn't doing much talking even to one of their own.

"Uh-huh. Good luck."

The moment he disconnected, Reece called his lawyer to brief him on the more public situation. Calling in to report to his agency would have to wait until he could be sure he wasn't overheard.

After checking with Mary, Reece learned he'd already booked their only cancellation for the night so he returned upstairs. He was standing by the bedroom window when Kelly exited the steamy bathroom dressed in a simple powder-blue nylon gown, rubbing at her wet hair with a white terry-cloth towel.

She came to a startled halt the moment she saw him. The spray of freckles stood out on pale cheeks. The brilliance of her eyes was dimmed by fatigue. She looked waif-like and so appealing Reece didn't dare move.

"Oh! I didn't realize you were back. I decided to take a quick shower."

Her words were choppy. Her eyes slid away from his as she busied herself with the towel. "Do they have another room?"

"No."

She hesitated a beat. "Your apartment's in D.C., isn't it? No one's killing people there."

"Not so far."

"Not funny."

"No," he agreed seriously, "it isn't."

She continued to rub at the wet strands of hair as if it were the most important task in the world. "But reporters will be looking for you there, won't they?"

"Us," he corrected, "and, yes, they'll have my usual haunts staked out. Relax, Kelly. I told you, I don't sleep with every woman I'm attracted to. I'll be back for you in the morning."

Her eyes flashed to his face. "Where are you going?"

"Someplace where you aren't such a temptation."

Her lips parted. Surprise made her blink. "Not funny." Her voice was uncertain.

"No, it's not. It's damn inconvenient, if you want the truth."

Color flared, dimming her freckles. He liked that she blushed so easily and suspected she hated the fact. Every emotion was clearly conveyed by her expressive features. Pleased that she wasn't immune to the growing attraction between them, he also knew this wasn't the time to explore what was happening.

"Reece, I don't want you to get the wrong idea here, but we aren't children and this is a big bed. You could... What?"

He stopped the upward curve to his lips just short

of a smile. "My fragile male ego isn't ready to hear that you consider me harmless."

"Harmless?"

"You were going to say we could share the bed but not each other."

It took a beat before her eyes narrowed in irritation. "Actually, I was going to suggest you could get a pillow and blanket from your friends and bunk out in the hall."

He couldn't help it. He laughed out loud. "You delight me."

"Really? Because you're annoying the heck out of me."

"I know. Again, sorry."

He crossed to her and lifted the towel from her hand, tossing it to one side. "I like you, Kelly O'Donnell." He ran a knuckle down her cheek, pleased when he detected an answering quiver. "I really like you. And, when this is all finished, we'll explore this attraction and see where it leads."

She sucked in a breath, laid her palm on his chest and pushed. Hard. He stepped back automatically.

"When this is all finished, Mr. Maddox, you'll have the house, not the builder."

Ruefully, he inclined his head. "Okay, that probably came out a little strong."

"Think so?"

"I apologize."

"You want to try for an even dozen?"

He tugged on his ear. "Pass. How about if I simply slink back out the door and see you in the morning before my tongue can dig the hole any deeper."

He kept forgetting that she didn't know him at all, while he'd known about her for years.

"Where will you go?"

Her instant concern was reassuring. "Downstairs. The Haverdocks are friends of mine. I don't see them as often as I'd like so we'll sit and talk for a while. They offered me the couch in their private quarters."

She shook her head and exhaled hard. "I'm shorter than you. And I'm not injured."

Touched by the implied offer he took the steps that closed the distance between them and raised her chin with a knuckle. Her eyes widened, but not in fear and she didn't attempt to pull back. He swore softly. "I guess I'll go for that even dozen, after all."

Her lips were incredibly soft. He kissed her tenderly and desire slammed through him when she kissed him back. Her hands reached for his shoulders, her soft weight leaning into his.

Reece stepped back before he could deepen the kiss. His voice came out husky with desire. "On second thought, I'm not sorry at all. Get some rest, Kelly. I'll be here when you wake."

ALLAN AND MARY were in the kitchen when Reece went downstairs. "I'll take you up on that couch, after all, but I have to go out for a little while."

"Do what you need to do. We'll keep the back door unlocked until you get back," Allan said.

"I owe you."

"No." He shook his head with a flat stare. "You don't."

Like others Reece had privately bankrolled, the couple felt indebted to him for a shot at their dream. They were good people. He did not want to bring trouble to their door. Bad enough that Gene was dead because of him.

A short time later, he let himself in through the back door of Custom Concepts. There had been no sign of anyone nearby, although he knew whomever Mark had assigned to watch the monitors would alert Mark to Reece's presence.

As he started to bypass his desk, Reece realized James Prince needed to attend to a few details if Reece wanted to continue to preserve the fiction of his existence. It might already be too late, but, for Kelly's sake, he spent the next several minutes dealing with the mundane tasks she'd left for him. The minute he finished, he went to her office for a quick look around.

Kelly was an orderly person. Everything was filed and clearly marked. He hadn't really expected to find anything and he didn't, but there was only one explanation for what was going on. Somehow, Gene had prevented the other side from finding the flash drive.

He would have made every effort to conceal the drive if he thought someone was on to him, but only if he was certain he couldn't shake free. If he'd stuck the drive in an envelope and mailed it to himself, Kelly would have found it.

Reece drummed his fingers against the desktop. How could he come out and ask her about the drive?

He couldn't, but James Prince could. For all she knew, it might be something of his.

If she had the drive and knew where it was. A big if.

Suddenly a man's voice called to him from the hall. "Reece?"

Reece relaxed. "Kelly's office."

Mark appeared in the doorway a second later. "Want some help?"

"I'm pretty sure what I'm looking for isn't here."

"You're looking rough, man."

Reece inclined his head. "Thanks."

"How's Kelly?"

"Asleep, I hope."

"Like you should be. I brought you a present." Mark crossed the room and placed a semiautomatic on the desk along with two clips and a piece of paper.

Reece stared from the man to the gun and lifted the paper. "What's this?"

"Permit to carry concealed. Don't worry, it'll be legal by the time anyone runs a check."

"You scare me sometimes, Ramsey."

"The same might be said of you, particularly after the fascinating conversation I had with a Mr. Smith this evening."

Reece straightened. Mark sprawled in a visitor's chair in front of Kelly's desk looking totally relaxed.

"He and another man wanted to come inside Custom Concepts and have a look around. I dissuaded them."

Reece swore. He slid the gun and clips into his jacket pocket. "Everyone parted in good health?"

Mark smiled. "More or less. After we got done posturing, Mr. Smith claimed to work for a set of government initials. He had a shiny ID badge and everything. He thought his badge would buy them admittance."

"Which is when you dissuaded them."

Mark smiled without humor. "Seemed like the thing to do. They wanted to come in and look for something, too. When I explained that wasn't possible they gave me a phone number. They suggested you call them after we talk."

Exhaling, Reece set his jaw and moved to the edge of his chair. "They're outside now?"

"No doubt. I think their equipment may be better than mine." Mark sounded annoyed.

With a soft oath, Reece lifted the receiver and dialed the number Mark recited. The call was answered immediately. Even if he hadn't recognized the voice, the coded phrase confirmed his identity.

"Any success?" the man called Mr. Smith asked.

"No."

"We'd like to ascertain that for ourselves."

Reece debated. He could tell them to take a hike, but he might need their help. "Back door's open."

Mark raised speculative eyebrows as he hung up. "Want to explain?"

"No, but this would be a good time for you to vanish."

"Right." Mark stood. "Try to stay alive. And get some sleep."

Mark ghosted away. Minutes later, Smith and his silent companion appeared.

"Ms. O'Donnell?" Smith asked.

"You going to offer her protection?"

"As I told you earlier, that's out of our jurisdiction." Reece clenched his jaw.

"But we'd like to talk to her," the man continued.

Reece stood and walked past them. "We don't always get what we want."

"Your cover is blown, Mr. Maddox."

He stared into the man's dark brown eyes. "Is this the part where you remind me that if I'm caught or killed the government will disavow any knowledge of me?"

Neither man smiled. "That information is important."

"And I'm not. Got it."

"The woman may have answers."

Hands balled at his sides. Reece forced them to uncurl.

"The woman's name is Kelly." He let his anger show. "She just lost her father because he tried to help me get that information to you. I want to know what happened to him."

Neither man spoke.

"Why cover up Arthur Weems's identity?"

An indefinable emotion slid across Smith's features and was gone. The temperature in the room seemed to drop several degrees. Reece forced himself to show nothing but anger in the face of that empty stare.

"You don't want to protect her? Then leave her alone. If she knows anything, I'll call. When this is finished, so am I. Be sure to lock up when you leave."

Turning his back to them was one of the hardest things Reece had ever done. He expected them to stop him from leaving. They didn't, nor did they make any move to follow. His mind raced. He had to force himself to walk slowly to his car. The moment he started the engine and pulled out, his cell phone rang.

"I cleaned your car," Mark's voice told him, "but if either of them touched you, you're tagged."

"They didn't."

"Then drive like the wind. They badly want to know where you're going. There were three devices in and on your car and I could have missed one. They'll double team you as soon as you pull onto the street."

"You just earned a bonus."

"I'll remember that. You know Tooey's Garage?"

"Yeah."

"There will be a red Maserati parked on the right. Key's under the mat. Leave your convertible. I'll see it's well cared for. A woman named Piper Briggs will meet you at Haverdock's back door with the cat."

"A suitably large bonus," Reece promised. "And I won't even ask where you got a red Maserati at this hour."

Mark was chuckling as he disconnected.

Chapter Seven

Kelly woke from a surprisingly dreamless sleep to the sound of purring. Opening her eyes, she found the room bathed in sunshine and one arm encircling a ball of silky gray fur. The cat sat up alertly when she did.

"What are you doing here, cat?"

Reece, of course. She couldn't believe he'd gone to her apartment last night and found the animal for her. It wasn't even her cat. Yet, there was no doubt that this was the stray she'd been feeding. The cat stared at Kelly with intelligent green eyes and pushed her nose into Kelly's hand. Automatically, she began to stroke the animal while it purred its contentment.

Reece's act of kindness nearly unraveled her. People didn't do things like that. But Reece had.

What else had he done?

She jumped out of bed, startling the animal into leaping away at her sudden movement.

Why had Reece gone back to her place? All that subtle flirting last night was second nature to him. She didn't believe for a moment he'd been serious.

Was he?

Did she want him to be?

"No! Of course not!" She crossed to the bathroom to discover a litter box and two bowls had appeared since she'd last been inside. Reece had entered the room while she'd been asleep and she'd never heard a thing. How was that possible?

She'd locked the bedroom door and put the deadbolt on. She knew she had. Of course, his friends had master keys to the room, but how was it she'd slept so soundly she hadn't heard a thing?

The champagne. Drinking wasn't something she did often. And she'd had a lot of champagne on too little sleep. Still, it was scary to think Reece could have done all this and she hadn't known.

The cat checked out the bowl holding the water, then nosed the empty bowl that held traces of some sort of wet food. It gazed at her expectantly.

"Sorry, cat, I got nothing. Go find Reece, he's the magic man."

Thankfully, it was Saturday. No one would be at the office. She could go to work in yesterday's clothes and no one would be there to notice.

Except yesterday's clothes were no longer hanging on the hook on the back of the bathroom door. Instead, there was a thick bag labeled Becky's Boutique in black-trimmed gold letters.

She forced her breathing to steady. There was no reason to panic. No doubt Reece had intended this to be another act of kindness. He was a take-charge sort of person. He couldn't know that she was, too, under normal circumstances. She didn't appreciate people treating her like some helpless female.

Stepping back into the bedroom she looked around, but her clothes were gone. Reece had left her no choice but to investigate the items in the bag or go storming downstairs in a borrowed nightgown.

Fuming, she discovered the plastic contained several outfits including bras and matching panties. There wasn't a price tag anywhere. The first item was a shimmery royal blue sheath that stole her breath. No way could she afford a dress like this. And where would she wear it in the first place?

Her fingers caressed the blue silk appreciatively before setting it aside. Sleek black slacks and a matching jacket were paired with her choice of a tailored blouse in pale cream with black piping or a soft, fitted sweater with a cowl neck in a deep hunter-green. Tempting, very tempting, especially the sweater. She touched it lightly. Definitely out of her price range.

The last item was a simple black jogging suit also trimmed in white and paired with a choice of a white boatneck tunic or a fitted mock turtleneck in black. While more her speed, she cringed at the thought of what the cost of these items would do to her bank account. Still, they were fantastic and she had to wear something.

The jogging suit and white top fit as if she'd shopped for them herself. Not that she'd ever enter a pricey shop like Becky's Boutique normally, but if clothes made the man, they also did wonders for a woman. She looked good. The blasted man had excellent taste.

Quickly, she braided her hair and coiled the braid on top of her head while the cat investigated everything and made a nuisance of herself.

She stepped into the bedroom and jerked to a startled halt. Reece smiled a welcome. On the dresser was a tray holding two steaming mugs.

"Good morning." His eyes lingered appreciatively. "Very nice."

"I'd like the receipt for this."

"Already paid for."

"My father taught me not to take things from strangers."

"We're hardly strangers. We've spent the past two nights together." He shrugged. "That's what the media's going to imply."

"All the more reason not to fuel their story." She folded her hands over her chest.

"You're going to be stubborn about this, aren't you?"

"I teach mules."

Reece sighed. "I believe you."

"You went to your apartment last night, too?"

"No. Why?"

She looked pointedly at his black jacket, white dress shirt and black slacks.

"Oh. I had these in the car." Thanks to Heath, who'd brought him several outfits yesterday. Reece followed her glance to the mirror over the dresser behind him. "Other than our hair colors I guess we do sort of look like Ken and Barbie."

She cocked her head. "You know what a pair of dolls look like?"

"I bought a set for my niece a few years ago." He shrugged. "Mary's friend did a nice job picking that outfit for you. It looks like it was made for you."

She ignored the compliment. "Mary's friend?"

"Did you think I picked out the clothes?" The touch of humor in his voice prickled. "I know better. I told you I have a sister. She's informed me on numerous occasions that I know nothing about women's fashion. So I left that task to Becky and Mary. Mary took your clothes to clean but said she couldn't have them back in time for you to wear this morning, so she suggested calling Becky."

"Did you have a parade through my room? Did you drug me?"

"No drugs and sorry if I overstepped, but you were exhausted from lack of sleep."

"Not to mention half a bottle of champagne."

"Yeah, well, I wasn't going to mention that part. Ouch."

The gray cat tried to climb his leg in a bid for attention. "Hey, there, little one, that hurts. Mary said she'd bring you up some breakfast in a few minutes," he told the small animal, lifting it so it could snuggle into his arm for easier stroking. "In the meantime, all I have is coffee."

"So you went to my apartment after telling me I should wait until today."

"Not guilty. I called and asked a friend to find the cat for you. I knew you were worried about her."

His sincerity left her at a loss for words. How could she stay angry when Reece was trying to be so kind? The cat certainly approved, and she was touched by his thoughtfulness. But the cynical part of her couldn't help wondering what he wanted for all this kindness. She hadn't forgotten the way he'd kissed her last night.

And as long as she was being honest with herself, she had to admit what made her so nervous was that she had wanted his kiss. She still did even though she sensed there was a lot more going on here than he was telling her.

Breakfast came with the room and Kelly let Reece convince her that Mary and Allan would be hurt if they didn't put in an appearance downstairs.

"I thought we didn't want to draw attention."

"That was before it mattered. Once we talk to the authorities, the media will be all over the story. They're going to want to know where you've been and I'm sorry, but I don't see a way around this one. For a positive spin, just think, we'll put Haverdock's on the map."

He was right, but she didn't have to like it.

Several sets of eyes followed them to a table in the main dining room. The whispering started before they were even seated. Kelly ate very little, letting him carry the conversation on his own.

"I'm sorry, Kelly. I know you didn't want your name linked with mine, but, for the next few days, you have no choice. I promise I'll do some damage control. Just stick with the story."

"I'm hardly worried about my reputation, Reece, but do you really think anyone is going to believe you came to a small company like Custom Concepts to have a house built?"

His gaze glittered with firm resolve. "Absolutely. Say it with authority, Kelly, because you *are* going to build me a house."

She hesitated. "All right. And why do we tell them we spent the night together?"

"We don't. We don't talk to them at all. That's what I pay my lawyer for. Unfortunately, they'll put their own spin on this due to the reputation they've created for me, but, if you don't want to add fuel to the story," he shot a meaningful glance around the room, "try not to look like I kicked your cat."

"She's not my cat."

Reece relaxed. "I believe she sees things differently."

"My apartment doesn't even allow pets."

"Mine does."

Her heart gave a funny little stutter. His eyes were serious and watchful. Once again, she thought of the desire she'd sensed in him last night.

"Then, you take her."

"How about I take both of you?"

Kelly couldn't seem to breathe as he leaned forward intently, lowering his voice.

"I have a three-bedroom apartment. Not only does it allow pets, it has twenty-four hour security. I'm offering you a safe haven until this all blows over."

Her mind spun while her pulse raced.

"If you really believe that your father's murderer is coming after you, then my place is safe."

"Custom Concepts has security," she managed, hating the sound of uncertainty in her voice when she'd meant it to sound firm and decisive.

"It's a warehouse."

She nodded. "With really good security. Reece, if he comes after me there, I'll have him on video. Then the police will have to pay attention."

"And they can play the video at your funeral."

She glimpsed real anger in his expression. As impossible as it seemed, she'd swear he cared about her. She hardly knew the man. Yet, there was something about Reece that made her feel safe.

He pulled a cell phone from his pocket and glanced down impatiently. She hadn't heard it ring, but his expression abruptly changed to concern.

"Excuse me a minute, Kelly. I think I need to take this call."

Reece stood quickly and crossed the room to the empty hallway. "Heath?"

"Listen, old man, there's been a dust-up here at the building. The police found a dead security guard in the stairwell outside your flat."

Fear gripped him. "What happened?" he demanded.

"There was some sort of scuffle. The guard ended up with a broken neck and no one heard or saw a thing. The security cameras on our floor had been disabled."

Reece forced his fingers to ease their grip on the cell phone. Before he could ask how Heath knew about the cameras, his friend continued.

"The media is camped outside. Our telephones are under siege and the local bobbies want to speak with everyone on our floor, particularly you."

"Why me?"

"They think the killer was trying to break into your flat."

Reece swore softly.

"Quite right. I second the sentiment."

"Did he succeed?"

"Not so far as I know. And I'm sorry to tell you that your lovely companion is no longer a secret. They're showing photographs of the two of you on the telly repeatedly, given this bit of business. Do you need anything? More clothing? A solicitor?"

"No."

"Right, then. I'll let you get back to whatever it is you were doing."

"Having breakfast."

"At this hour?" Heath managed to sound appalled. "She's all wrong for you, you know. Next thing she'll be picking out a cottage and you'll be changing nappies."

Reece met Kelly's worried gaze across the room. "There are worse things."

"I'm going to pretend you didn't just say that and go back to bed."

Reece hesitated and then returned to the table. His thoughts tumbled chaotically. "We need to leave."

Kelly stood immediately. He placed his hand in the small of her back, needing that small physical contact with her.

"What's wrong?"

He paused out of sight of the dining room. "Later. Would you put the cat in the carrier while I make our apologies to the Haverdocks?"

Her lips tightened, but, meeting his gaze, she nodded abruptly and climbed the stairs without further protest. He headed for the kitchen to speak briefly with Allan and Mary. When he entered the bedroom a few minutes later, Kelly looked rumpled and disgruntled.

"Problem?" he asked as she finished snapping closed the carrier.

"Your cat doesn't like to be caged."

He nearly smiled and went into the bathroom to gather up the bag of clothing. "I'll take her if you'll carry these."

"I can't afford these clothes."

"Then, it's a good thing I already paid for them."

"So you wear them."

She was going to be stubborn. Reece took a breath and forced himself to relax. "Kelly, there are no strings attached here. You helped me the other night when most people would have called the police. I offer these to you in return for your kindness. You may refuse, particularly if you don't like them, but—"

Her eyes slit in warning. "You don't owe me hundreds of dollars worth of clothing."

"I'll be the judge of what I owe you, Kelly O'Donnell." He met her stormy eyes and let her assess the truth of his words.

"Fine," she agreed after a moment, anger in every syllable. "As long as you consider the debt paid in full, then thank you."

He didn't correct her assumption. She had no idea how much he owed her. In the kitchen, Mary handed her another hanger with her old clothes, now cleaned and ironed. As Kelly hugged Mary, Reece added more thanks to hers. Minutes later, they were outside.

"What's this?" she demanded as he stowed the clothing in the small trunk.

"What?"

"This isn't your car."

He'd forgotten. "I switched cars last night."

"Because you think this fancy red car is less noticeable?"

He had to smile at her expressive outrage. "It belongs to a friend of mine. No one will be looking for us in this car."

She handed him the carrier while she climbed in. "Maybe not, but I'm pretty sure everyone will be looking *at* us in this car."

"And all they'll notice will be you. Fasten your seat belt."

"Does that line actually work?" she asked with pursed lips, clicking the belt into place.

He handed her the carrier, then leaned down and planted a light kiss on feather-soft lips before either of them realized his intention. She gazed up at him with a soft "oh" of surprise.

"I like you, Kelly O'Donnell. We'll argue later."

"About what?" she demanded.

"Pretty much everything, it seems."

THEY DIDN'T SPEAK AGAIN until Reece pulled into the underground parking lot of a tall structure in D.C.

"This is an office building."

"Yes, it is. My lawyer's office is upstairs."

Her heart hammered in her chest as he parked the car and turned off the engine. "Why are we here?"

"My attorney arranged for the police to meet us here."

Cold settled in her belly. "Why?"

"A security guard was killed outside my apartment last night."

Kelly shivered.

"It's nothing to do with us. There are a number of wealthy people living in my building and it appears the guard stumbled on some enterprising thief who'd disabled the security cameras. They got into a fight outside my apartment and the guard fell down the stairs and broke his neck."

Scared, she was also angry in the face of his calm expression. "You know it was no coincidence. If the police learn you were stabbed outside my place the night before…"

"The situation would be awkward," he agreed.

Kelly drew in a deep lung full of air and released it slowly. "What were you really doing there?"

"A gentleman never tells."

She let the seconds stretch. He didn't take his eyes from hers, but his expression told her nothing.

"I could tell you I work for a secret government organization and I was there waiting for someone."

She swallowed an angry retort.

"Or I could tell you I had too much to drink at an after-premiere party and some friends of mine thought it would be a good joke to dump me in a strange neighborhood and see if the media would catch wind of the story. Only I got attacked and you rescued me and the joke turned out not to be funny, after all."

That explanation fit a lot better than anything else he'd said so far.

"Is that what happened?"

"It certainly fits my image, doesn't it?"

His flat tone didn't quite mask the hurt she sensed behind his question. She wasn't sure why he cared what she thought of him, but absurdly, she knew that he did.

He *had* been drinking that night. She remembered smelling the alcohol on him at the time, although he hadn't seemed drunk. Of course, getting stabbed would be enough to sober anyone pretty quickly. And, in truth, the media would have had a field day with the story.

If it was the truth.

"You're good at evasion, aren't you?"

This time he waited her out. Kelly scowled when it became apparent that he wasn't going to elaborate. Did it really matter why he'd been there?

"What do we tell them when they ask how we met?"

His shoulders relaxed fractionally. "Would you be willing to tell a little white lie?"

"How little?"

"It would look better if we said I called you a week ago to discuss the possibility of building a house for me. We could say we met for dinner last Tuesday evening to discuss the situation."

"What about phone records?" He had no way of knowing that Tuesday night she'd waited in vain inside Custom Concepts for a glimpse of the elusive James Prince.

"I doubt they'll check, but, if they do, I'll deal with it. Don't worry. We can tell them we've been meeting quietly because we didn't want to draw the attention of the press. We were at Haverdock's last evening and spent the night."

He waited with a blank expression.

"Together?"

"That would be the implication, yes. Don't volunteer anything. Don't pad the story or offer details. Remember, we're the victims here. We'll let Ray handle most of the talking."

"Ray?"

"Ray Hubbard. My attorney."

"Of Hubbard and Associates?"

"Yes. Why? Do you know them?"

"My partner uses this firm."

"Good choice," Reece agreed easily. "They're one of the top firms in the D.C. area. Several people I know use them."

The cat gave a pitiful wail.

"All right, Reece. There really isn't much choice, is there?"

He exhaled heavily, climbed out of the car and came around to the passenger side to take the carrier. "I'm sorry, Kelly. I'll do what I can to minimize the situation."

"Whatever you were really doing outside my apartment, I'm sorry you got involved in my personal problems as a result."

THE INTERVIEWS with the lawyer and then with the authorities went smoothly. They listened when Kelly insisted the dead man outside her apartment was somehow connected to her father's murder, but they weren't enthusiastic. They seemed much more intent on tying the two events to Reece.

Kelly marveled at how cool and relaxed he appeared. Nothing they said or did rattled him in any way. He was courteous and appeared eager to help without giving them a single thread to use. Reece told his story of how the two of them had met and made everything sound so reasonable that even she wouldn't have questioned him.

Kelly had no opportunity to ask the lawyer about James Prince, but she suspected he wouldn't have told her anything, anyhow. The lawyer was as smooth as Reece. She felt disheartened when they left a few minutes after the police.

Reece paused to set the cat carrier down before they stepped into the garage itself. Without seeming to, he effectively barred her way while he studied the scene beyond the glass doors. Her heart rate accelerated when one hand went to his jacket pocket.

"What are you doing?"

"Making sure the press isn't waiting for us." His gaze swept the area.

"Are you planning to shoot them if they are?"

Startled, he looked at her. Kelly glanced meaningfully at the hand in his pocket. He withdrew it leaving behind a distinct bulge she hadn't noticed before.

"You are! You've got a gun!" She was suddenly frightened.

"I have a permit to carry concealed. I'm a target, Kelly. Rich and famous also means painting a bull's-eye on your chest. Like yours, my dad believed we should be prepared and able to take care of ourselves."

"How do you know what my father believed?"

His reply was smooth and unperturbed. "I've watched the way you move. People who've had strong martial arts training move differently. And you're an only child."

"I don't remember telling you that I was an only child."

"You didn't. You told the police. Come on. The cat's been in this cage long enough."

The cat let out a mew of agreement. He lifted the carrier and shoved open the glass door. Kelly said nothing, not even when he handed her the carrier and proceeded to go over every inch of the outside of the car. He paused near the bumper to flick something onto the ground before sliding behind the steering wheel.

"What was that all about?" she asked.

"One of the tabloids put a tracking device on the car. Don't worry about it. It happens all the time."

"Aren't they expensive?"

He smiled without humor. "That's why I backed over it."

"I thought you said they wouldn't know this car."

"Someone must have seen us pull in. I should have considered that they might have my lawyer's office covered."

"You have to be kidding! How can you live like this?"

He shrugged. "It's always been this way."

Neither of them said anything further until they were out of the garage and onto the main street.

"Why did you tell the authorities I'd be staying with you? I could stay with Leah or one of my other friends tonight."

He lowered his gaze from the rearview mirror to glance her way. "If a killer is coming after you, do you really want to endanger anyone else?"

"Of course not, but what makes you immune?"

His gaze returned to the rearview mirror. "I can afford to hire security."

"I've already accepted the clothes, Reece. You don't owe me anything more."

"No, but I want you to build me that house, Kelly. I've got a vested interest in keeping you alive."

The cat mewed unhappily.

"You need a name for your cat," he said.

"She's not my cat and you're changing the subject."

"Yes, I am. How about Bonus Eventus?"

Kelly inhaled, but Reece was watching something in the side mirror. "What kind of name is Bonus Eventus?"

"I'm pretty sure she was the Roman goddess who affected single events. No wait—Bonus Eventus was a god, not a goddess. He had something to do with profit and trade. Maybe a good harvest?"

"You studied roman gods and goddesses?"

Reece shrugged and offered her a teasing grin. "Doesn't everyone?"

"No. And that's a ridiculous name for a cat even if she was a he, which she's not."

"Okay, how about Pellonia?"

"What was she the goddess of?"

"I don't remember if she was an actual goddess. I think she was married to Saturn. I'm pretty sure she was a protector who drove enemies away."

"Of course she was. What, no goddesses who protected a man from a knife-wielding crazy by fetching help, huh?"

His grin widened. "Specifically? Not to my knowledge."

Kelly eyed the carrier. The cat returned her stare. "Pellonia, huh? Well, if she doesn't object, who am I to tell you what to call your cat?"

"Don't listen to her, Pellonia. Underneath that hard exterior is a woman who loves you. What do you think of your new name?"

The cat closed her eyes in either acceptance or

dismay. Reece's gaze returned to the rearview mirror. There was tension in the set of his shoulders.

"What's so interesting back there?"

"We've picked up a tail." His jaw hardened. "Hang on to the carrier. This could get interesting."

Chapter Eight

Without warning, Reece veered left, cut off a pickup
truck and guided them smoothly, if insanely, across
three lanes of traffic to catch a left turn signal
already turning yellow. Kelly held her breath as
they sped through the intersection, made a second
left through the next light directly in front of an
oncoming truck and left honking horns in their
wake. Her breath caught again as Reece made a
third left turn onto a one-way street. Oncoming tires
squealed. She braced for impact as the cut off
drivers protested with more horns and raised digits.
The next traffic light stopped them cold.

Reece studied the traffic. Kelly was about to
protest that she'd rather the tabloid ran a picture of
them alive than dead when, without warning, he
pulled through the red light and into the intersection.
Afraid to scream out loud, she screamed silently as
a stretch limousine barely missed them and a Toyota
stood on its brakes to avoid smashing into the limo.

Reece appeared unconcerned. He dodged traffic with incredible calm, steering the car across the busy roadway until he reached the right-hand lane. He made a sharp right turn at the same intersection where he'd originally turned left. Halfway down the block he made an abrupt U-turn in front of two lanes of oncoming traffic and pulled to the side of the road to park in front of a fire hydrant.

"You okay?" he asked.

"I'll let you know when my voice catches up."

He grinned. "I think we lost them."

"I'd hate to think my heart attack was for nothing."

His warm gaze melted something inside her. "You're a special lady, Kelly O'Donnell. Most women would have screamed."

"I did. It just got jammed inside on my sheer terror. Besides, I didn't want to distract you."

With a wide smile, he cupped the side of her face lightly before turning back to study the flow of traffic in front of them.

"Do you mind telling me why we're sitting here? Not that I'm complaining, you understand. I'm all in favor of not moving anytime soon."

"I want to be sure they didn't follow us."

"Reece, Jeff Gordon couldn't have followed us. I'm not sure my stomach followed us."

The quicksilver grin came and went again while his eyes remained on the busy street. "I'm thinking you had a point about staying at my place. It may not be such a good idea. I'll drop you and Pellonia off at Custom Concepts. Then I'll grab some carryout and bring it back so we can discuss our options."

"Options?" She pinched the bridge of her nose against a building headache.

"We need a place to stay where we won't be hounded."

"Then, why are you taking me to Custom Concepts? If you'll recall, the press found us there first. And homing device or not, this car will stand out like a lantern in our lot. It's Saturday. The company trucks and my dad's pickup truck will be the only vehicles parked there. This fancy little toy car won't exactly blend in."

"Not to worry. The trucks have been sitting there all this time so they aren't a problem and we'll just park this car inside the warehouse. You have plenty of space in your loading area and we can spend the evening designing my house."

"You're planning to sleep there?"

He considered for what seemed like a very long moment, then shook his head. "No, you only have the one couch and concrete's not very yielding. I suppose it would do in a pinch, but we'll play this by ear, for now."

"Hold it right there! Who put you in charge?"

"Experience. Okay, I think we're clear. Three light changes should be enough."

Kelly glared at him, but he wasn't even looking her way. "For what?"

"To make sure whoever it was didn't figure out what I did."

"Even I'm not sure what you did."

Again with the grin that somehow managed to cut right through her annoyance.

"Don't worry about it. While we're at the warehouse Pellonia can take care of your mouse problem."

"The warehouse doesn't have a mouse problem!"

KELLY SAT AT HER DESK watching Pellonia chase a brightly colored plastic ball around the room while she waited for Reece to bring some Chinese carryout back for dinner. She'd pretty much decided she'd have better luck arguing with the cat than the man.

Leah had called and left messages on her cell phone and her office phone. Probably her home phone, as well. Kelly didn't call her back. She was still debating about asking her friend for a bed for the night.

Her cell phone began to trill again, bringing the inquisitive feline running to stare at her purse. Kelly fished it out, stared at the word *unavailable* and answered.

"Ms. O'Donnell?"

Kelly straightened. As always, his voice sounded

distorted, but there was no question as to her caller's identity. "Mr. Prince."

"You are all right, then?"

"Yes, of course."

"There is no of course. I was distressed to hear about the incident at your apartment."

Kelly wasn't sure how he managed to convey sympathy and censure at the same time, but she stifled a sigh. "I wasn't home."

"So the media stated."

Definitely censure. She should have called him. Probably Fred, as well. Her foreman would be worried by all the news stories, too.

"They are saying you were in the company of Reece Maddox."

Her spine stiffened. There was still censure in his tone and she had to control an urge to take out her frustration on him.

"Mr. Maddox wants us to build a house for him," she explained crisply. "This could put Custom Concepts right up there with the big firms. Wait until you hear the details."

There was a long pause. "I see. Do we have a contract, then?"

Kelly deflated. "Verbally, yes. We're still in the discussion stage of what it is he wants."

"I see. And how is our injured employee?"

Guilt hit her hard. "I don't know," she admitted.

His silence condemned her. "I've spent half the day with Reece's attorney and the authorities." She hated that she felt obligated to explain anything to this irritating man. "I'll call the hospital now and see how he's doing."

"The paperwork—"

"Will be on your desk, ready for your signature tomorrow," she assured him.

She should have remembered to call the hospital to check on Louis even though Fred had no doubt stopped by. She was the boss. It was her job, even if she had been a little busy. Irreverently, she supposed she could have called the hospital between oncoming cars as Reece sped through D.C. Obviously, the stress of the past few days was making her punchy.

Or Reece Maddox was. She shook her head and forced herself to concentrate on what James Prince was saying.

"Monday will be soon enough," he stated calmly.

For what? She'd already lost the thread of the conversation. Oh, yes, the paperwork.

"I have another matter I need to discuss with you," he continued.

"I can't wait." Oops. The pause on his end gave her time to grimace. She needed to focus here.

"This is important, Kelly."

"I'm listening."

"Very well. I'm searching for a flash-drive unit

your father had in his possession shortly before he died. You know what a flash drive is?"

For an instant, she was tempted to play dumb and tell him no just because he irritated her so much when he took on that paternal tone. Only, this time there was an underlying edge to the question that made her frown.

"I know what a flash drive is, Mr. Prince, but Dad used zip drives."

"This wasn't his, it was mine."

A prickle of unease marched down her spine.

"The drive contains some important information that I need. It's a little red and silver sticklike device. You're certain you haven't seen it?"

"What sort of information?"

"Nothing you need to be concerned with. Have you come across it in anything of your father's?"

A cold, half-formed thought chased chills up her spine. "I haven't gone through all of my father's personal belongings yet, but I'll be happy to look for it when I get back to the apartment."

"You didn't find any packages or envelopes in the post office box that you haven't opened yet?"

"No." Her heart began to beat more rapidly as the thought began to solidify into a certainty.

"What about packages or envelopes waiting to be mailed?"

"Sorry, Mr. Prince. It was probably in the trailer

when it caught fire. Does this drive have something to do with my father's death?"

"Hardly."

But he'd hesitated a beat too long, as if surprised by her question. Or was he also wondering if there might be a connection?

"Mr. Prince, I need to see you."

"That won't be possible."

"You're going to have to make it possible. Mr. Maddox is insisting on meeting with you as part of his contract." The audacity of the lie surprised even her.

"Is that so?" he murmured after a slight hesitation. "Then, you'll need to explain to him that I don't meet with our clients."

"I have. This is a large deal, Mr. Prince. The largest one Custom Concepts has ever had. You can understand why someone in Mr. Maddox's position would want to know the people he's dealing with."

"But he won't be dealing with me, will he?"

"It's your firm, too." Unfortunately. And she was more resolved now than ever to change that status.

"If it comes down to a deal breaker, Ms. O'Donnell, perhaps we don't need the man as a client."

That dropped her jaw. "You'd turn down a multimillion-dollar deal rather than meet with him?"

"Let us hope it doesn't come to that. If you come across the flash drive, please give me a call immediately. Good evening, Ms. O'Donnell."

Stunned, Kelly sat there holding the open cell phone several seconds after he disconnected. All this time she had let Leah kid her about James Prince being a vampire and she had never once considered that he might be evil in another way.

That her Midnight Prince and his mysterious flash drive might have had something to do with the death of her father had just become a serious possibility.

"NOW THERE'S a chagrinned expression."

Reece snapped closed his cell phone and regarded Mark balefully. "Kelly wants to introduce me to myself."

Mark grinned widely. "This should be interesting."

They both stared at the monitor that showed Kelly at her desk, drumming her fingers against the surface, a look of concentration on her face.

"Oh, the schemes we weave when first we practice to deceive…or words to that effect."

"I don't need mangled Shakespeare, Mark. I just screwed up. Now I need a workable plan."

"And I'm supposed to provide one?"

"No. You're supposed to listen to me rant. But, for the money I'm paying you, if you've got a plan I'm all ears."

"First, I'd need to know what's going on."

Reece blew out a breath. "No, you really don't. Suffice it to say I need to find a missing flash drive and I pushed her too hard." Kelly was rooting around in a filing drawer.

"For Smith and his nameless partner?" Mark guessed.

"Yes."

"In that case, I don't want to know what's on that flash drive. Is she right? Is this why her father died?"

Reece scowled. Mark already knew more than he should. "He was doing me a favor."

"And the other dead guy?"

"That's a question I'm going to demand an answer to just as soon as I can find a place to stash Kelly."

"Uh-huh." Mark looked pointedly at the monitor. Kelly was dialing the telephone.

"What?"

"I don't think you're going to find stashing her so easy to do a second time, Reece. You want my opinion? Tell her the truth."

"That's your plan?"

"Nope, just a recommendation based on observation. The woman's intelligent and she wants her father's murderer to pay. In her shoes, I'd be focusing all my attention on James Prince right now. In fact, I'd be asking for police help in tracking him down."

"That's all I need."

The telephone rang on his desk. Mark picked it up. "Yes, Vince. Who did you say?" He shot Reece an amused glance. "That's what I thought you said. Put her through."

He covered the mouthpiece. His wry grin was mocking. "I was wrong. Kelly isn't going to call the police. She decided to hire me, instead. And Vince said to tell you that they just delivered your carryout up front."

Reece opened his mouth, but Mark hit the speaker button and spoke formally. "Mark Ramsey."

"Mr. Ramsey, this is Kelly O'Donnell."

Reece groaned under his breath.

"Your firm handles security for Custom Concepts."

"Yes, Ms. O'Donnell. I recognize your name. What can I do for you?"

Reece stared at her uncompromising expression on the monitor. She was looking directly into the secreted camera in her office.

"Does your firm handle investigative work as well as security systems? And, if not, could you refer me to someone who does?"

Reece shut his eyes.

"That depends, Ms. O'Donnell. What sort of investigative work are we talking about?"

"I have a silent partner who calls himself James Prince. I need every scrap of information you can get on him, especially a photograph."

REECE TRIED NOT TO SHOW any reaction when Kelly told him what she'd done, but Mark's laughter was still echoing in his head. He couldn't believe Mark had agreed to look into her case.

"Would you rather me, or someone she hires out of the phone book?"

"Tell me there's a third option."

Mark had started grinning. "Marry the girl and tell her the truth when your first grandchild's born."

That the situation was his own fault didn't make Reece feel any better. He was almost grateful when his cell phone rang as he sat with her over Chinese carryout trying to think his way out of this dilemma.

"Excuse me a minute, Kelly. It's my friend, Heath. I'd better take this call."

Kelly picked up a spring roll and resumed eating as he greeted his friend.

"You haven't forgotten tonight's party, am I right?"

Reece swore softly.

"Yes, I thought a reminder might be on order," Heath added smugly.

"I haven't been back to the apartment."

"And you don't want to be doing that, either. A pair of our favorite tabloid sods are mucking about outside. Want me to nip over and bring you a suit?"

"No, I think I'd better pass on the party, Heath."

"Not a chance. You promised me moral support

after I helped haul your bony arse out of trouble in Italy, remember?"

Reece remembered.

"I'll bring you a suit. You and your lady can ride with me. We won't stay long, but my Mum'll have my hide if I don't pop over and at least say hello to my cousin. One drink and we're clear."

Reece sighed. He had promised, but he knew better than to believe it would simply be one drink and a quick escape, despite the fact that Heath was no fonder of these formal affairs than he was.

Aware of Kelly sitting across the table listening, Reece turned his attention to her. "Hold on a minute, Heath. Kelly, would you go to a party with me tonight?"

She was already shaking her head before he spoke. "I can't."

"Mary tossed a dress in with the other items, didn't she?"

"Yes. And it will look fabulous with my dirty work shoes." She glared at him.

"What size shoe do you wear?"

"There's more to it than shoes. I don't carry makeup in my purse and then there's my hair."

"Your hair is lovely and you don't need makeup."

"Flattery will get you nowhere. It's impossible. I can't go to a party tonight."

"Heath promises we don't have to stay long and I did tell him I'd go with him."

"Fine. The two of you go and leave me out of this."

"Let me talk to her, Reece," Heath insisted in his ear.

Grimacing, he passed the phone across to her. "Heath wants to talk to you."

"I don't even know Heath."

"Your good luck's about to change."

With a scowl she accepted the cell phone. "Hello?" After a moment of silence she regarded Reece with a humorous twitch to her lips. "He said to tell you he heard that."

Reece closed his eyes. He knew his friend. If he wanted to, Heath could convince a saint to stroll through hell.

"Thank you, but no, I'm sorry. Did you say the British Embassy?"

Reece kept his eyes closed despite the panic that crept into her voice.

"I can't go to— I don't care if it is only a reception… So what if he's your cousin? I don't even know you… No. Absolutely not. What? I thought the two of you were friends…"

He opened his eyes. No doubt, Heath had just invited her to go and leave Reece behind. She sputtered a laugh at something he said. The sound was magic. He realized he'd never heard Kelly laugh before. Annoyed that it was Heath and not him who'd drawn that laughter, his jaw tensed.

"Do you practice being outrageous?" she was demanding as color moved up her cheeks.

There was now speculation in the gaze she turned back on him.

"None of your business. I'll take care of my own shoes, thank you very much."

Reece sighed. They were going to the embassy reception. Good thing they'd just eaten. There would be canapés, but very little in the way of real food at this thing. It was going to be a long night.

Abruptly, she held out the phone. "You talk to him. He won't take no for answer."

"Don't I know it. Kelly, the thing is, I did promise. Heath did me a favor and I owe him and you might find it fun."

"It's the British Embassy!"

"We'll only be in the rotunda. It's nothing to get all nervous over."

"Your friend said they had to move the party because of a leak in the rotunda. It's going to be at a private residence in McLean."

"Well, there you go, then. It's a house party."

"With the British ambassador!"

He had to smile. "He's actually a very nice person."

She rolled her eyes. "You know him."

"Guilty as charged. Please, Kelly. I know it isn't

how we planned to spend the evening, but I'd really appreciate it if you'd go with me. Think of the opportunities you'll have."

"Opportunities?"

"To get Custom Concepts out there to a whole new group of people." He'd hit the right note. He saw it in the sudden flare of interest in her eyes. "These sort of affairs are all about networking. There will be people there you'll find it well worth your time to get to know."

"But I'd need to go to my apartment and get—"

"No. After what happened to that cameraman there's bound to be all sorts of press still hanging around. We can shop for whatever you need. There's time."

"No. I'll call Leah. She has more shoes than some department stores and we wear the same size shoe. Your phone is squawking."

Relieved to know he'd won, Reece put the cell phone to his ear once more.

"I do not squawk," Heath protested. "Nevertheless, I think I'm going to like her."

"Forget it. I have plenty of time to tell her what you're really like before she meets you."

And now Reece was thinking this might work out well. The party would buy him some time to figure out what to do with her tonight to keep her safe.

LEAH GAZED AT KELLY with rounded eyes bordering on awe. "That dress is beyond cool," she breathed. "Where did you get it?"

Kelly smoothed the slinky material with her hand. The sheath fit as if it had been designed for her alone. The vibrant blue color deepened the blue in her eyes. Leah had fussed with her hair, brushing it within an inch of its life, and convinced Kelly to pull the sides up and leave the back flowing long and free. And, of course, Leah had the perfect pair of strappy slender heels to go with the dress. Their bold blue color was nearly an exact match.

"I bought them to go with a dress for a party," Leah told her. "They didn't match *my* dress half so well. This is so cool. I can't believe he's taking you to an embassy party."

"Neither can I. What made me think this was a good idea?" But she knew. She enjoyed being with Reece, far too much for her own peace of mind. Seeing him in his own element, so far removed from her lifestyle, should help stuff any lingering fantasies back where they belonged.

And this *was* a once-in-a-lifetime opportunity to get her company name out to the sort of people who could put Custom Concepts on top and keep it there.

"Be careful with your hands," Leah was admonishing. "I'm not sure that polish is dry yet."

"It's dry."

"Okay. Whatever you do, don't eat anything that can ooze or crumble tonight. Don't drink any liquid that isn't clear and stay away from anyone holding a drink and waving their hands."

"Thanks a heap."

"I'm just saying. Do you know what it costs to have something like that dress cleaned? You don't want a glass of red wine to ruin it the first time you wear it."

"Okay. Anything else, Mommy?"

Leah made a face and then laughed. "My black cape should work for a coat. I don't have anything else dressy enough to wear over this."

"I don't need a coat."

"It's starting to rain outside. I just hope the cape will look fancy enough."

Kelly glanced at the window and saw that Leah was right. Large raindrops splattered against the panes of glass. "Reece said not to fuss."

"Reece is a guy. Guys never fuss. They just toss on any old suit and… Oh. Oh, wow. Okay, I take it back. That is not any old suit."

Kelly followed her friend's gaze down the hall where Jimmy was letting Reece inside the apartment. "Oh."

"Yeah. He must have fussed. Guys aren't supposed to look *that* good in a suit."

"You're drooling."

"Only a little. I'm trying not to pant."

"It's still just a suit." One that fit Reece like it had been tailored for him. And it probably had been. She was so out of her depth here. Her mouth went dry. What was Eugene O'Donnell's baby girl doing with such an impossibly handsome international playboy? And going to an embassy party, of all places. This was beyond insane. Nothing good could come of this evening.

But, looking at that strong male profile, she knew it would take a major catastrophe to stop her. Maybe, just for tonight, she could pretend there wouldn't be a price to pay for this. Just for tonight, she would pretend she was someone else. Flirt a little, smile a little and mingle with the sort of people that made the society pages of the newspapers.

Who was she kidding? Disaster lay straight ahead.

Heart pounding, Kelly lifted her chin, straightened her shoulders and walked down the hall to meet her Titanic.

Reece turned. The momentary heat in his eyes went a long way toward boosting her flagging confidence. "You look incredible."

His gaze made her feel incredible. She shushed the voice in the back of her mind that called for caution. It would only be a couple of hours. How bad could things get?

REECE DECIDED to drive, so Kelly didn't meet Heath Brockmorton until they had parked among dozens of other expensive cars that lined the McLean, Virginia street of outrageously pricey homes and started toward the brightly lit windows of a large brick two-story. Heath and his companion met them on the walkway leading to the front door. He was every bit as handsome as Reece, his blond good looks a sharp contrast to Reece's darker, mysterious aura.

Heath's companion was a gorgeous brunette he introduced as Rebecca Holliman. She proved so genuinely nice that it was hard to be intimidated by her spectacular looks. To Kelly's surprise, instead of a model, Rebecca turned out to be a graphic designer for a prestigious advertising firm. Kelly liked her instantly.

Kelly tried for nonchalance as the four of them passed through the formal receiving line in the vast, marble foyer. She welcomed the warmth of Reece's reassuring touch as he guided her along. He and Heath seemed to know everyone in the reception line and Heath greeted his cousin jovially, promising to wait until the man was free to chat.

Then they were moving along to make room for others crowding inside. The men led them past an elegantly appointed and rather crowded formal living room and down a few steps into a classically decorated family room—fit for a family of fifty or more. Appropriate seeing as there were at least that many people already inside the room and more just about everywhere she looked.

Tuxedo-clad waiters and waitresses circled with trays of appetizers while a crowd gathered around a makeshift bar in one corner. One entire wall of glass windows and doors looked out on a gigantic deck and what appeared to be a mature forest stretching behind the house. Lightning rippled across the sky, adding a counterpoint to the festivities.

Reece brushed his lips against her hair. "Something to drink?"

Kelly blushed. Heath and Rebecca appeared not to have noticed. "Please." The men disappeared into the crowd.

"Is it always like this?" Kelly asked, gazing around.

"Awful, isn't it?"

Someone bumped into Rebecca, nearly spilling a full tumbler of something on her ivory dress. She gripped the man's arm to steady him. "Oliver?"

"So sorry." He balanced his drink before it sloshed to the floor and rocked back on his heels. His handsome face split in a charmingly boyish smile. "Rebecca! At last, a familiar face! And such a lovely one at that."

"Hello, Oliver. I'm surprised to see you here."

"Frankly, I'm surprised we don't see everyone we know here given all these people. A lady friend of mine works for the embassy."

"Of course she does."

He grinned unrepentantly. "I'd introduce you, but I seem to have lost her somewhere. Please tell me you're here unescorted so I can flatter you all evening and the night won't be a total waste."

Rebecca laughed good-naturedly. "Heath and Reece went to get drinks. The guest of honor is Heath's cousin."

He sighed dramatically. "Figures. So that makes this incredibly stunning redhead Kelly O'Donnell."

Kelly tensed despite Oliver's flirtatious smile.

"Ah, don't look so worried. There was no crystal ball necessary. I saw your picture with the infamous Maddox on the news last night. Welcome to the strange world of the rich and famous where no one and nothing is private from the stalking paparazzi."

His wry tone offered commiseration as he took her hand in his and introduced himself. "I'm Oliver Kendall, one of the many followers of the rich and famous because, alas, my father lost most of our fortune some time ago. Have you known our wealthy friend long?"

He stroked the back of her hand as he released it.

The touch was courtly rather than sensual and she found herself relaxing. "Uh, no. Not really."

"Good." His smile widened. "Then, there's still a chance for me to woo you from his arms."

"What about your friend from the embassy?" Rebecca asked.

He waved a dismissive hand. "She'll understand. I was drawn to the flame of this gorgeous hair and…"

Reece appeared, handing Kelly a fluted glass of bubbly liquid. "And, if you don't want to get burned, Kendall, you'll keep right on moving."

There was an undercurrent of real warning in the words even though Reece spoke lightly. Kelly wasn't sure if she should be flattered or annoyed by his hint of possessiveness.

"Looks like we arrived just in time, Reece," Heath added before she could decide, handing Rebecca a flute of white wine. "Oliver is on a mission to charm every woman he meets."

"And why not?" he demanded good-naturedly. "Women are endlessly fascinating creatures and I live in hope that one of them will take me way from all this. Some of us must rely on charm. Not all of us were born to a fancy accent and a title," Oliver complained with good humor.

Watching the men, Kelly decided they also found it hard to be annoyed by Oliver. He didn't seem to take himself or anything else seriously.

"You have a title?" she asked Heath.

"Of course he does," Oliver answered. "You're what, ninety-sixth in line for the crown?"

"Ninety-eighth," Heath corrected with an imperious swish of his hand.

Rebecca winked. Kelly wasn't sure if Heath was teasing or not. There wasn't time to ponder the issue as she became conscious of Reece's hand resting lightly against her back once more. She took a quick sip from her glass, trying not to feel unnerved, and was surprised to find sparkling water rather than champagne.

Reece leaned his head toward her ear. "They were using cheap champagne." His eyes twinkled with shared humor.

"In that case, good choice," she murmured self-consciously, all too aware of the others watching and listening despite their continued conversation.

Their banter was interrupted when the guest of honor made his way over to them. Oliver slipped away and, after a few moments, Reece deftly guided Kelly away, as well. They joined another knot of people he knew.

"Curtis."

"Reece!" The older man turned and exchanged handshakes as introductions were made. He took Kelly's hand firmly. "I was very sorry to hear about your father."

"You knew my father?" Shocked, she stared at the man. She knew, beyond a doubt, that she'd never seen him before.

"We only met in passing, but I liked him."

Reece interrupted to continue with the introductions before she could ask how someone as obviously wealthy as Curtis Long could have met her father.

The others were all business people of means and, while more than one appeared to recognize her name from the news reports, no one made any mention of it. They were far more interested in discussing some recently proposed legislation that would affect business owners everywhere.

Kelly found herself joining the rather heated discussion while discretely watching the man called Curtis Long. His age was right, though his voice was all wrong. Still, she'd always suspected James Prince used some sort of device to distort his voice.

Had she finally come face to face with her mysterious partner?

Chapter Nine

Curtis and his wife drifted away before Kelly could broach the subject of her father again. She didn't want to embarrass Reece or call more attention to herself, so it seemed wisest to bide her time until she could work her way back over to him and ask a few pointed questions.

The house continued to swell with people until they spilled over into most of the downstairs rooms. She quickly lost track of Curtis Long, but Reece had been right about the sort of contacts she was making tonight, so it was some time before she realized that Reece and the people he was talking with had joined another circle.

He hadn't gone far and he caught her eye the moment she started to look for him. The warmth of his gaze stirred an answering heat inside her. No man had ever done that to her before. He raised his glass in question and smiled when she shook her head at his offer of a refill.

When, a short while later, a hand pressed against the small of her back, she turned expecting to find Reece. Instead, the man called Oliver Kendall smiled at her.

"Have you been abandoned, already?"

"Not really. Reece is right over there."

Automatically, her gaze sought him in the crowded living room where they had migrated a short while ago. As if sensing her look, Reece raised his head and their eyes met. Reassured, she smiled to let him know all was well. He winked and turned to respond to the man standing beside him.

"Pity," Oliver said. "However, I'll seize these few minutes alone to tout all my virtues."

"You have so few it will only take a matter of minutes?"

He covered his heart dramatically with the hand not holding a half-full glass. Humor glinted in his eyes. "I'm sliced to the quick."

"I have confidence in your survival skills."

His warm laughter invited intimacy. He stepped sideways, effectively cutting her off from the group she'd been conversing with.

"You're really quite lovely, you know?"

"Do you flirt with every woman you meet?"

"Well, yes, but it's the simple truth."

He swayed slightly. Kelly realized he was holding himself together with the control of someone who'd had quite a bit to drink but hadn't reached the point of sloppy drunk yet. In contrast, his eyes seemed completely alert, almost watchful.

"So are the two of you really an item or is that all media hype?" His hand stroked her arm lightly.

Kelly stepped back against a chair to let another couple pass between them without making it obvious that she was pulling free of Oliver's touch.

"Media hype," she assured him, scanning the crowd.

Reece had crossed into the dining room where a large table brimmed with food. She spotted Heath talking with two men she hadn't met yet. One had his arm in a sling and was looking her way with disturbing intensity.

Kelly cursed the media coverage that had placed her in this uncomfortable spotlight and looked away from the trio.

"How did you come to know the infamous Maddox?" Oliver asked. "No offense, but you really aren't his usual type."

She dragged her attention back to him and decided to ignore his comment about type. "Infamous?"

"In certain quarters, absho...absolutely."

"I'm building a house for him."

Oliver's eyebrows rose. "You, personally?"

"My crew," she amended.

"Ah. I'm impressed, but not really surprised that

a woman as lovely as you would have an entire crew of men ready to do her bidding."

"Uh-huh." His flattery was so outrageous Kelly found it hard not to like him.

"So that's how you met?" he persisted.

The lie they'd decided on tripped easily off her lips since it was at least partly true. "Reece approached my firm to build him a house."

"I like the way you say 'my firm.' I think I'm falling in love here."

"Don't let that worry you. It's probably the alcohol. You'll feel better in the morning."

Oliver laughed out loud. "You really are amazing. No wonder Reece is so taken with you. And here I was going to warn you off. I think he's the one who should be warned."

"Warn me off?"

"He generally sticks to the sort of women who understand the score. I was afraid you didn't but I see I was wrong." The hand dropped to her arm, once more. "I like you, Kelly. Will you marry me?"

She pulled her hand free gently and shook her head. "Sorry. This lifestyle's too rich for my blood. It's a nice place to visit, but I wouldn't want to live here."

He laughed again.

"Do you know Curtis Long?"

Obviously startled by the question, Oliver met her

gaze full on. In that instant, Kelly was certain he was as sober as she was. Unease slithered down her spine.

"We've met. Why?"

"I was just wondering. I understand he's in import-export."

His gaze narrowed. "Why do you want to know about Curtis?"

She didn't know what she'd said wrong, but there was a disturbing intensity to his tone that sent her gaze skimming past him in search of Reece. It was Heath who saved her from a response by appearing at her shoulder.

"Is Oliver making a pest of himself then, Kelly?"

Instantly, Oliver's easygoing mask slid back into place. He waved the hand holding his glass, spilling a few drops.

"When have you ever known me to be anything other than witty and charming, Brockmorton? I was just about to ask the lady if she'd like another drink. It appears that Maddox has abandoned her to the fate of an empty glass." He wiggled his own dangerously.

"Steady on, there. Where is Reece?"

Kelly shook her head. "I'm not sure." A scan of the crowded dining room didn't reveal him, although it was difficult to see clearly past the press of bodies all around.

Oliver shrugged. "He'll turn up. Reece is nothing

if not depressingly proper. In the meantime, what are you drinking, beautiful lady?" He lifted her empty glass, taking it from her hand.

"Sparkling water."

He shuddered. "Now there's something to rust your insides. A woman as lovely as you should only drink champagne."

"Water, if you please."

"Ah, one of those stodgy designated-driver types, eh? Have it your way, but don't say I didn't warn you about the dangers of H2O. I'll be right back. Don't let the limey woo you in my absence with his honeyed accent. I'm thinking of adopting one myself just to compete."

Watching him saunter off, only the slightest bit unsteadily, Kelly felt as if she'd just had a reprieve. "Is he always like that?"

"Worse, as a rule. I've poured him into a cab more than once, I'm afraid, but he's harmless." His gaze continued to work the crowd.

Kelly thought Oliver wouldn't appreciate being considered harmless by someone he so clearly envied, but she kept the thought to herself. Maybe she had misread the past few minutes. She was starting to get a headache.

"Did you lose Rebecca, too?"

Heath took his gaze from the crowd and smiled at her. "No. She's talking to some friends in the family room. I came to collect you and Reece. Since duty's been satisfied, I'm thinking we should make good our escape while we can. I thought the four of us might stop for coffee and pudding before calling it a night."

"Pudding?"

"Dessert to you Yanks. Why don't you wait in the foyer by the front door so I don't lose you in the crowd? I'll collect the pair of them and join you there."

"All right." The truth was, she was ready to call it a night. Curtis and his wife had disappeared completely before she had the opportunity to question him and she'd begun to suspect it had been on purpose. She'd have Mark Ramsey look into Mr. Curtis Long first thing tomorrow.

The storm was making another pass over the area and the sound of renewed thunder was clearly audible in the large foyer. Four people stood near the hallway. Otherwise the space was empty.

Kelly relaxed for the first time all evening. She wondered what the butler had done with all the coats.

Without warning, every light in the house went out. She sucked in a sharp breath as ominous black nothingness closed in around her. There were startled exclamations, some nervous laughter and raised voices.

"Stay where you are everyone." A British voice carried over the crowd. "The storm must have knocked down power lines again. I'll get a torch and light some candles so we can carry on. Just stand still a moment."

Kelly smiled. No one could possibly see well enough to do anything other than stand still. The house was wickedly dark. She literally couldn't see her hand in front of her face. The main door was only a few feet behind her, but totally invisible.

The chatter inside rose with a nervousness created by the intense darkness. Kelly heard footsteps on the hard marble floor.

"Reece?"

There was no answer, but someone had entered the foyer with her.

"Who's there?"

She sensed motion a second before a hand snaked out, fumbling to cover her mouth. She was so stunned at first that she didn't even struggle. Yanked against a firm, masculine body, she was dragged in the direction of the front door. Fortunately, her assailant couldn't see any better than she could. They bumped against the wall. Years of self-defense training kicked in.

Bringing the sharp point of her stiletto heel down on his instep, Kelly twisted. He inhaled in pain but his grip merely tightened. His hand found the front door and flung it open.

Kelly reached up with her free hand, clawing for

his eyes. He blocked the attempt and yanked her through the door and into the night. Panic threatened to reduce her to victim status, but her dad's voice echoed in her head.

Panic's a worse enemy than your attacker. You know what to do.

As rain pelted them, all but blinding her, Kelly let her body go completely limp. He wasn't prepared for the sudden pull of weight. He stumbled, loosening his hold.

Kelly twisted free and screamed. The sound was lost in a clap of thunder. She lashed out with her foot, aiming for his kneecap. The dress was too tight. She caught his shin instead. He reached for her.

Abruptly, he was wrenched backward as a second blurred shape spun him about. Instinctively, she backed away. Her heel caught on the edge of the sidewalk and she stumbled and fell to the grass.

A well-placed kick doubled over her rescuer. Kelly pulled off a shoe to use as a weapon and scrambled to her feet. But, instead of reaching for her again, her attacker sprinted down the driveway.

"Kelly!"

She spun back around. "Reece?"

He straightened in pain. "Are you all right?"

"Yes." She swiped at the water running down her face. "How bad are you hurt?"

"Come on."

"Wait! Leah's coat is still inside."

"I'll have Heath retrieve our coats. We need to go."

There was no arguing with that tone, nor did she want to. Sopping wet, she was starting to shiver both with cold and reaction. She slid her shoe back on and saw that Reece had something in his hand.

"You've got your gun?"

"Yes."

"You couldn't have pulled it out sooner?"

She saw a flash of teeth as he smiled. "Sorry."

Shivering, she accepted his other hand when he reached for her. Together, they ran down the driveway with rain lashing them. Reece held the gun ready, watching alertly, although what he could see in the strobe effect caused by the lightning skittering across the sky, Kelly couldn't have said. She couldn't see a thing in the blinding darkness that gripped the world.

They'd parked the Maserati halfway down the block and fear accompanied her every step. Her attacker could be anywhere, lying in wait for them with his own weapon. Reece moved stiffly. That kick had probably reopened his wound, but he was tense and alert.

"Shouldn't we call the police?"

He didn't slow. "Is that what you want to do?"

The impact of what had happened was just now starting to hit her. "Someone tried to kidnap me."

He squeezed her hand. "They didn't succeed."

"Thanks to you." She began to tremble in earnest. "How did you know?"

"I didn't. I was talking with Rebecca when Heath said you were in the hall waiting to leave. The lights went out and I went to find you. The front door was standing open."

His tone was grim. They reached the car and he opened the passenger door. Kelly laid a hand on the side of his face.

"Thank you."

"I shouldn't have left you alone. Get in."

She slipped inside. The shaking was worse now. Reaction. Someone had tried to kidnap her.

Reece slid behind the wheel. His features were taut and his eyes were never still as he continued scanning the dark street. She didn't know how he'd be able see enough to drive in this torrent of blustery rain.

"Reece, how did anyone know I was there tonight?"

"Good question." The gun had disappeared. He started the engine with a wince.

"You're hurt!"

He shook his head, pulling onto the street with a speed she normally would have considered reckless.

"I'm good."

"No, you aren't."

"Kelly…."

She ignored the warning in his tone. "You mean,

if I unbuttoned your shirt I wouldn't see blood on the bandage?"

"If you unbuttoned my shirt, I don't think either one of us would be thinking about blood."

The words were dry, meant to tease, but liquid heat fluttered to life low in her belly.

"How can you even think about sex right now?"

His lips curved. "I'm a man. I always think about sex."

"Liar."

He shook his head. "I've been wanting to peel you out of that dress all evening. And that was before it got wet and took on the aspect of a second skin."

She glanced down. The material had molded itself to her and cold had puckered her nipples into tight buds. They showed so clearly she might as well have been nude. Kelly crossed her arms over her chest to cover them.

"How could you possibly notice something like that in the dark?"

"I told you, I'm a man."

"Well, I'm not that easily distracted by a manly chest," she managed.

"I can't say the same about yours. And, I assure you, I'd be more than a little distracted by your hands on my skin."

She had to work to steady her racing heart.

"You're starting to sound like Oliver." Her voice wasn't as steady as she would have liked.

"I am *nothing* like Oliver."

"No, you aren't. Although, he isn't as superficial as he pretends."

Reece's mood changed once more. "What do you mean?"

Surprised by the intensity of his tone she shook her head. "Nothing sinister. I just meant he uses charm and flattery as a cover."

They came to an abrupt stop behind a line of cars waiting to clear an intersection where the traffic light was out. Reece turned to face her. "What sort of cover?"

There was nothing teasing in his tone now. Kelly picked her words carefully, not sure what to make of his attitude. Surely, he didn't think it had been Oliver who'd grabbed her. It couldn't have been.

Could it?

"Oliver is jealous of you and Heath. He jokes about being allowed to hang with you and your friends because of his personality, but I suspect there's some serious resentment under all that charm."

"Who grabbed you, Kelly?"

"I don't know, it happened so fast. Between the dark and the rain…" She shivered.

Reece reached over and switched on the car's

heater. "I shouldn't have left you alone," he repeated.

"Please, adult woman here. I don't need anyone to hold my hand. At least, not usually," she added ruefully, remembering how grateful she'd been for the touch of his hand a few moments ago.

"I enjoyed the party. I like Heath and Rebecca. And you were right about the sort of contacts I made tonight."

He relaxed slightly, although, the moment he cleared the intersection, he resumed driving with almost reckless speed along the slick streets.

"No one could have known I was going there tonight, Reece. Even I didn't know ahead of time."

"No. They couldn't have. I think someone seized an opportunity."

She waited, but he didn't add anything. "Okay, I feel like an actor in a play who doesn't know her lines. Clue me in here: Why did someone just try to kidnap me?"

"Aside from the obvious, you mean?"

"Don't even go there. Rapists don't sneak into parties hoping to find a woman standing alone that they can attack."

"No, but someone bent like that could have been in attendance and seized on an opportunity when the lights went out."

"And I could be a famous movie star, but I'm not."

"You want to be a movie star?"

"Funny man. You aren't what you seem be on the surface, either."

He went very still. Suddenly, that seemed like a dangerous thing to have said.

"Nice to know you don't find me superficial."

She studied his profile, uneasy, but not afraid. "You're dodging again."

A tic in his jaw began to jump. "What do you want me to say, Kelly?"

"Let's start with the way we met."

"I explained that."

"You know better."

He started to protest and stopped.

"Thank you. I don't like lies."

Reece gripped the steering wheel more tightly. "I don't like telling them."

"But you aren't going to tell me what you were really doing outside my apartment that night, are you?"

Silence filled the car. Even the windshield wipers seemed muted.

"Fine. What's the deal with Heath?"

He whipped another startled glance in her direction. "What do you mean?"

"I don't know what I mean. I didn't get a copy of the script, remember?" She summoned anger to cover the nerve-racking fear hovering in the corners of her mind. Someone had tried to kidnap her. That fact was just starting to sink in. And this incredibly handsome man was keeping secrets. "At least we can rule out Heath."

"Unless he had a coconspirator."

"You're joking! You suspect your friend?"

He relaxed marginally. "Not really, but I'm not ready to write anyone off at the moment."

"You're serious."

He offered no reply.

"You should call him. Heath will be wondering what happened to us. And I want to make sure we don't leave Leah's cape there. She'd kill me."

Better to concentrate on the mundane, because otherwise she was going to lose what little control she had left. Kelly shivered hard despite the growing warmth of the car.

Reece steered into a brightly lit gas station and she realized the roads in front of them were no longer dark. He parked before an empty pump and pulled out his cell phone. Punching in a number, he spoke the moment someone answered. "Heath?"

"Where the bloody hell are you?"

His voice carried to where Kelly sat huddled against the chills wracking her body.

"Kelly was feeling ill." Reece's voice was smooth and calm. He apologized to her with his eyes. "Do me a favor and grab her cape and my coat when you leave, will you?"

"Is Kelly all right?"

"She will be." Grimness edged his words, but there was a promise in the gaze he fastened on hers.

"Where are you? Do you need help?"

"No. Thanks. Make our apologies, will you? I'll call you tomorrow." Reece closed his cell phone. "I don't think you should go back to Leah's tonight given what just happened."

"I wasn't planning to. Good thing we left everything except this dress in your trunk."

He gave her a questioning look.

"My uncle keeps a boat in Annapolis."

Reece remembered. He'd seen pictures of her and Gene on the *Money Pit,* as it was named. He hadn't considered the boat as a haven, but it was an excellent choice. It belonged to her uncle by marriage, so it wasn't registered to an O'Donnell if anyone went looking.

"My aunt and uncle are in California visiting friends, but I have a set of keys."

"And the cat?"

Her expression told him she hadn't even thought about the animal.

"It's okay," he continued. "We left her with plenty of food, water and litter. She should be fine for one night. She's got the whole warehouse to explore."

"Even invisible mice to chase." She managed a small smile. Reece thought he'd never seen anything more beautiful.

"We'll go to the marina."

"Weren't you the one who told me earlier I should wait to be invited?"

Lightly, he stroked the side of her cheek.

"Invite me, Kelly."

Chapter Ten

"Awfully used to getting your own way, aren't you?"

There was no animus behind the words, so Reece smiled. "I go after what I want."

Kelly's eyes glistened in the reflected light. "So do I." And she opened the car door and stepped out.

Reece filled the car with gasoline while Kelly used the restroom to change out of her wet dress and into the jogging suit again. He was smiling as he traded his wet suitcoat for the jacket in the trunk when his cell phone rang.

"You two all right?" Mark demanded.

"Fine."

"Sorry. My operative saw the altercation in front of the house, but she wasn't close enough to intervene. That won't happen again."

"Thanks, Mark. Did he get the license plate?"

"Stolen from an SUV. *She* stayed with you rather than chase after the car."

"Okay. We're heading to Annapolis. Kelly's uncle has a boat there. The *Money Pit*."

"I'll let her know. No one tampered with the Maserati, however, I'm thinking you might want to exchange it for something they won't recognize."

"Not right now."

"No. Leave your keys in the glove box. I'll get it switched tonight. I've got a silver-gray Ferrari."

"You never cease to surprise me. Thanks, Mark."

The rain had lightened considerably when Kelly reappeared, and so had his mood. With Mark's people watching his back, the odds of having an undisturbed night just climbed. He handed her the cup of hot chocolate he'd purchased along with some other items inside the mini-mart.

"I thought you could use something warm to drink," he offered.

"You're a mind reader. I can't seem to stop shivering."

"It's early spring yet. This rain is cold and you got pretty wet, Kelly."

"You think?"

The rain was tapering off, but lightning still streaked the sky, followed by rumbles of thunder chasing after it as the storm moved away. They drove in companionable silence for several minutes while she sipped the hot beverage gratefully.

Reece was amazed by her resilience. Probably, he

should have expected her to take the attack in stride. She was Gene's daughter, after all. Unfortunately, that meant she was going to ask questions. A lot of questions. It was only a matter of time.

"How well do you know your friend, Curtis Long?"

That was one question he hadn't been prepared for. "He's a business acquaintance of my grandfather's. I've known him and his family for years. Why?"

"He really is an importer?"

Surely, she didn't think Curtis had tried to abduct her. The man he'd fought had been much younger than Curtis Long. But that wasn't to say the attack couldn't have been on his orders.

"Yes," he replied thoughtfully, "it's a family business."

"How would my father know someone like that?"

His fingers tightened on the steering wheel. He didn't know whether to be relieved or concerned by the direction of her thoughts. He hadn't expected to see Curtis there tonight, although, once again, he probably should have. Curtis did a lot of business with the British.

Once he had seen the man, there'd been no way to avoid the meeting and introduction and Reece hadn't seen any way he could ask Curtis to conceal Reece's connection to Kelly's father. He'd waited nervously for her to find an opportunity to talk privately with Curtis, but the opportunity hadn't presented itself by the time the Longs left, early. He'd considered that a boon from Lady Luck at the time. Now, he wondered about their hasty disappearance.

"Maybe your dad knew his son," Reece replied cautiously. "Steve wants to be a builder."

"That doesn't explain how Dad knew either one of them."

No, it didn't. He needed a diversion. "What's worrying you, Kelly?"

"I think Curtis Long may be my mysterious partner, James Prince."

Stunned once more, Reece stared at her intently. It had never occurred to him that she might think Curtis was James Prince.

"You could have your private investigator check him out," he suggested. At least, if Kelly sent Mark looking at Curtis, Mark would have an excuse not to be looking too closely at Reece.

"I intend to. How's your injury?"

Wryly, he shook his head. "It stopped bleeding."

"I'll take a look when we get to the boat."

Despite the dark confines of the car, he saw that she blushed. She was remembering what he'd said about her hands on his skin. He smiled. "I'd appreciate that. Warmer now?"

"Subtle, Reece."

"I was only wondering if I could turn down the heater," he told her mildly.

"I'll do it."

She leaned forward. Her hair covered her face, but he was sure it flamed redder than her hair. As soon as she sat back, Reece turned on the radio. Soft jazz filled the car. After a few minutes, Kelly began to relax.

Reece kept a close watch for tails, but didn't see even the one Mark had on them. Of course, the rain and the dark made it easy for someone to go undetected.

The rain had stopped by the time Reece reached the harbor. Kelly said nothing when he removed a change of clothing for both of them from the trunk.

"What's in the other bag?" she asked.

"Coffee, milk, juice and a package of doughnuts for breakfast."

He waited for a protest, but she merely led the way to where the *Money Pit* was berthed. The twenty-seven-foot powerboat rocked as they boarded. Reece told his stomach to behave. He'd swallowed the Dramamine tablets he'd also purchased at the gas station while Kelly was changing clothes. He reminded his stomach that he refused to be sick in front of her.

She unlocked the small cabin and turned on the lights. On the left, was a table with two built-in seats. The right side housed a cabinet with a tiny sink, a burner and a miniscule refrigerator. The steering panel sat in front of that with storage under the seat. Straight ahead and down two steps lay a padded sleeping berth and a small lavatory. Everything was neat. And compact. Extremely compact. His six-foot-two-inch frame filled much of the available space only inches from Kelly.

"Cozy."

She didn't look at him, but indicated he should stow the milk and juice while she took the clothes from his hand and hung them on a hook inside the bedroom wall.

"I don't imagine this is the sort of boat you're used to."

"Because it isn't a yacht?" She turned and he took the step necessary to close the short distance between them. "You think I'm that shallow?"

"I don't think you're shallow, at all. Let me get the first-aid kit."

"In a minute. There's something I need to do first." Before she could form the question, he reached out to frame her face. Her eyes went wide, but she didn't draw back as he lowered his face. "Kiss me."

"You're stalling," she breathed against his lips.

"So are you."

Answering humor glinted in her eyes. She slid her hands around his neck and melted against him. Her lips were incredibly, deliciously soft. Her eyes fluttered closed and, instinctively, he pulled her closer, savoring the heady feel of her in his arms at last. His mouth moved over hers, sampling her with a slow thoroughness that left them both breathing hard.

"You taste like hot chocolate."

Her eyes opened. He saw answering desire, but she braced a hand flat against his chest when he would have kissed her again. "First-aid kit."

"Has anyone told you, you have a one-track mind?"

"Frequently."

"My wound's fine."

"Ah."

He cocked his head, puzzled. "Ah, what?"

"I told you grown men run from the sight of me with a first-aid kit. Learned that lesson, did you?"

Reece found an answering smile. It was going to be all right. She wanted him. "Bring it on."

She stepped back and he took off his jacket while she pulled out the kit. Rain began to patter at the windows once more. The boat rocked gently. His stomach did the same without the gentle part and he commanded it to behave.

"You need to take off your shirt," she said.

"I see. Just a ploy to get me out of my clothes, huh?"

"Of course. I work in construction. I'm doing a comparative analysis of men's chests."

Humor danced in her blue eyes, but her gaze

followed his hand to the top button. It occurred to him that he'd done a lot of things with a number of women, but he'd never deliberately undressed for one while she watched his every move. It was oddly disconcerting, yet, arousing at the same time.

"Kelly, if you keep staring at me that way, I'm going to embarrass both of us."

"Are you forgetting I've seen it all before?"

"Not quite all."

Her gaze dropped lower.

"There's something different about the rest of you?"

"I like to think so."

Her grin was pure imp. "Of course you do. Men have such fragile egos."

"Shattered many of them, have you?"

"Nope. I leave the shattering to others."

"Glad to hear it." He pulled his shirt free and shrugged out of it. Her gaze fell on the bandage and her eyes narrowed.

"I knew he hurt you with that kick."

A splotch of bright red stained the white and a bruise was forming around the area. He knew there was more than one bruise from that brief encounter.

"Unlucky blow."

"I told you this needed stitches when it first happened."

"It only opened a little."

Lightly, she touched another bruise higher up on his chest, then she was all business as she set to unwrapping the gauze pad taped over the knife wound. He tried not to flinch when she dabbed hydrogen peroxide on the reopened cut.

"Okay, a manly *ouch*. I think you enjoy using that stuff."

The smile flickered and didn't reach her eyes. "Was the man tonight the same person you fought with at my place?"

"No. How could it be?"

She raised her eyes to his. "He knew right where to place that kick."

"Coincidence."

"I don't think so. No one has any reason to come after me. Except my father's killer. And he'd want me dead so I'd quit stirring up the police. The man tonight wasn't trying to kill me. I think he wanted to use me to get to you."

Reece swore softly as she began taping a fresh gauze pad over the wound. "He would have been right, Kelly."

She looked up in question.

"I'd do anything to keep you safe."

He could see his words had rattled her. Patting the last piece into place, she set the tape on the table without meeting his gaze. There was color in her cheeks. "Why?"

Reece lifted her face and covered her lips with his own. She went still. Then her arms crashed around his neck and she kissed him back with surprising fervor. His hands slid to her buttocks. He pressed her even closer, fitting against her with fierce need.

"Reece." She trembled in his arms. "Wait."

He groaned. "Please don't tell me you're going to send me away tonight."

Her laugh was shaky. She planted a kiss along his jaw. "I wouldn't send anyone out into that storm."

The boat rocked to remind him of where he was.

"We just need to go more slowly," Kelly told him.

"You're trying to kill me."

"Blood isn't sexy, Maddox. If you get blood on my aunt's sheets, she'll kill both of us. Take off your pants."

"What about yours?"

Her smile was pure seduction. "First things, first."

"Haven't we played this scene before?"

Pure mischief in her eyes. "Think you can stay awake this time?"

"I'll try. I'll really, really try."

But, when she gently pushed him down on the sleeping pad and lightly kissed his every bruise before making her way down his chest, he thought he might just die from the pleasure. And, when she finally straddled him, it took monumental control not to lose himself in the tight, slick warmth of her right then and there.

Sometime later, they woke to a sadistic explosion of thunder to find the boat rocking hard against its tethers while the storm raged overhead. Reece's stomach lurched. But, as she turned toward him once again, all thoughts of queasiness faded in the pleasure that was Kelly.

KELLY WOKE TO MORNING LIGHT filling the upper cabin and her breast filling Reece's hand. His body was pressed spoonstyle against her own. His erection stirred against her buttock and his finger began toying with a nipple.

"Again?"

He pulled aside a swath of her hair to nibble on her neck. "If you insist."

They laughed gently and she shifted to allow him better access. Only after they lay utterly spent, her head pillowed against his chest, did Kelly let herself consider the full ramification of what she had done. She wasn't the type to take sex lightly, but she'd thought she was mature enough to have a simple, enjoyable affair without entangling her heart or her emotions.

How could she have been so foolish?

Reece would walk away. Maybe not soon, but eventually. How could he not? People didn't fall in love in a matter of days. And a single night of sex didn't equate to forever-after. That only happened in books. People did, however, fall in love with their doctors, their rescuers, even their captors. She was pretty sure there was a term for that.

Dependency?

Her backbone stiffened.

"Something wrong?" Reece smoothed her hair with his hand.

"Just a cramp." No need to mention it was her heart constricting in pain. "I need to use the facilities."

"I know the feeling, but I'm not sure I can move. You wore me out."

Quickly, she rolled over and looked down at his bandage. She'd forgotten his injury. All that exertion couldn't have been good.

"It doesn't look as if it started bleeding again. How do you feel?"

"Besides being thoroughly exhausted, you mean?" The teasing left his eyes. "I'm fine, Kelly."

"You always say that." She started to get off the bed, but his hand snaked out and grabbed her arm. His gaze was soft with concern.

"Regrets?"

He was so handsome, so caring, so impossibly perfect. She touched his face, lightly scraping her fingers against the early morning bristles along his jaw. How could something so silly be so endearing?

"No, Reece. No regrets." She wouldn't allow them. Not now. The regrets would come later when she had to say goodbye. "But I really need to use the bathroom."

"So do I. Go."

Getting ready in such tight quarters should have been awkward, but wasn't. She added *considerate* to Reece's many other attributes. He'd disposed of the used condoms by the time she rejoined him and they managed to dress, put clean sheets on the berth and return the room to its pristine condition without bumping into each other.

Kelly made coffee with her aunt's tiny coffee-maker and took one of the chocolate-covered doughnuts Reece offered.

"Aren't you having one?"

"Uh, not right now."

"Is something wrong?"

He swallowed a tiny pill with a sip of coffee. She couldn't have said why, but, suddenly, she was pretty sure she knew what the pill had been for. "Do not tell me you get seasick."

"Wasn't planning to."

She covered the start of a smile. "Reece, we aren't even moving."

"Tell that to my stomach."

"We just spent an entire night on board. The boat was even rocking during the storm."

He held up a hand. "Don't remind me. I had you to distract me, then."

"I'm still here."

"And I'm very glad of that."

"Well, I was going to suggest going out on the bay for the afternoon if the weather was nice, but—"

He held up a hand. "I'll be fine. Just give the pills a chance to work. I'll take our clothes out to the car."

"Reece, I need to go back to Dad's…*my* apartment. I need to check the mail and messages and I want to take a shower and put on my own clothes."

"Those are your clothes." She held his gaze. Reece sighed. "Not just yet, Kelly."

"Why not?"

"I need to check with some people, first."

"Who?"

The pause lasted so long she thought he wasn't going to answer.

"The government agency I work for."

The words didn't make sense. And then, abruptly, they did. His watchfulness, his fighting and driving skills, his inability to tell her what was going on. All those little things added up to one incredible possibility. One she'd dismissed as a joke when he'd suggested it before.

"Are you saying you really are a spy?"

Reece held her gaze. "In a manner of speaking."

"I'm using English, what about you?"

"Was a spy. I quit. My connections gave me a unique opportunity to be helpful to our government from time to time. I could collect information where it was hard for them to place another agent."

"And, now that you've told me this, you have to kill me?"

"No, Kelly. My goal has been to keep that from happening to you."

Something cold slithered around in her belly. "Why me?"

"Bad timing. You took me in when…something went wrong," he concluded lamely. "That centered attention on you."

She hugged her arms. "That cameraman killed outside my apartment—"

"Was another innocent bystander. At a guess, he took a picture of the person who broke into your apartment."

She shivered. "And the security guard outside your place?"

"Someone wants information they think I still have."

"What information?"

He smiled with bitter humor. "If I told you that, *then* I'd have to kill you."

"That isn't funny."

"No, it isn't." He started to reach toward her, but

lowered his hand without completing the motion. "I'm sorry, Kelly. I never wanted you to be involved in any of this."

"Whatever *this* is."

She felt angry all out of proportion to the situation. She wasn't even sure why she was angry, except that she didn't want him to stand there looking at her with that mix of sorrow and regret. She wanted answers. And she didn't want to hear that the man she'd just spent the night making love with was a spy.

"You do work for...my government, right?"

"Yes, Kelly. I work for *our* government."

"Okay. Just give me a minute. This takes... I need a minute."

"I'll take our clothes to the car."

"And the dirty sheets. I'll need to get them washed and returned."

Reece nodded. He scooped up the linens and their clothes from the day before and headed outside. The sky was crisp and clear. It might not be full spring yet, but, in another hour or so, this marina would likely bustle with people. There were already a few of them moving toward the docks from the parking area.

He pushed thoughts of Kelly from his mind as he surveyed the scene. If someone wanted him out of the picture, this was the perfect opportunity. His skin prickled as he walked to the parking lot imagining a riflescope trained on his head.

Several early morning boaters nodded or offered a greeting on their way past, but no bullet whistled out of the air to rid the world of one Reece Maddox. Where the Maserati had been parked last night, a silver Ferrari now sat. The driver's door was unlocked. The key was where Mark had told him it would be.

He continued to scan the parking lot, but couldn't pick out Mark's agent, even though he knew the person was nearby. Placing everything in the trunk, he pulled out his cell phone and called Mark.

"I need a safe place to stash Kelly for a few hours. Maybe a couple of days."

"Trouble in paradise?"

His hand clenched around the plastic.

"You'd be fine out on the bay," Mark suggested.

Possibly safe, but definitely not fine. There wasn't enough Dramamine in the world for fine.

"I can't stay with her. She's going to be calling you for a rundown on me as well as Curtis Long. She thinks he's James Prince."

Amusement laced his voice. "And you want me to do what?"

"Give her the public stuff on me and whatever you can dig up on Curtis."

"It's your tab. And your funeral when she finds out."

"I told her I work for the government."

"That's more than you've ever told me."

"Mark…"

"Yeah. Okay. Is she going to let you stash her?"

He hadn't considered that. "Probably not."

"My license won't stand against a charge of kidnapping."

"It won't come to that."

"We are talking about Kelly O'Donnell, here, aren't we?"

Reece shut his eyes. He opened them on another sigh.

"Custom Concepts is about as secure as you're going to get, Reece."

"They know it's her place."

"But they won't know she's in there." His voice was stubborn. "I can make sure no one gets inside. Besides, her cat looks lonesome. I could put an operative in with her. Tell her you arranged for a bodyguard."

And wouldn't she just love that? "No. Not there. Come up with someplace else."

Mark sighed. "You don't want much, do you? Okay. I'm leaving the office now to meet someone for lunch. I'll see what I can come up with for both of you on my way."

"Make sure it has two bedrooms."

"That bad, huh?"

"I don't think Kelly's happy that she slept with a spy."

"Uh, Reece? She's holding on my other line," Mark told him.

"Go ahead. I have another call to make, anyhow."

Reece disconnected. Before he could dial the number for the dry cleaners a familiar figure came striding in his direction. Lips pursed, Reece met him halfway.

"Smith," he greeted.

"Let's take a walk."

Reece didn't argue as they began strolling amid the parked cars.

"Ms. O'Donnell is well?"

"No. I dumped her body overboard."

His expression didn't change. "I need to talk to her."

"No."

The other man's silence was pregnant with warning. Reece stopped walking and faced him.

"She doesn't have a clue about what's going on. She doesn't have the flash drive, hasn't seen the flash drive and can't imagine what her father would be doing with a flash drive."

"You've developed an attachment." The words were an accusation.

"I'm going to marry her." He heard the words and realized he meant them. Assuming they both survived the next few days, that he could convince her that he was serious and that she was willing to marry a wealthy playboy turned spy. Ex-spy.

He shook off the troubling list of arguments she could make. "In the meantime, I plan to do everything in my power to keep her safe."

There was nothing to be read in Smith's expression. "She may know something she doesn't realize she knows. The airport tapes showed the exchange being made in full view of the camera and everyone else around them. Prior to his greeting, Mr. O'Donnell, Curtis Long and his wife were in conversation with a fellow passenger by the name of Oliver Kendall."

"I know Oliver." Reece dismissed the man with a wave of his hand. "He's part of the regular fringe group. He was at the Italian party and so drunk Heath and I had to load him in a cab. I'm surprised he made it to the airport in time for his flight in the morning. Was there anyone besides Arthur Weems watching the exchange?"

"No one we've been able to identify so far. Eugene O'Donnell stopped by a restroom on his way out the door. He was out of camera range for eight point two minutes. Weems was in and out in under five."

Reece stiffened. "Gene didn't pass that drive to Arthur Weems."

"We've been working to identify every person who went inside before and after O'Donnell," Smith continued without comment. "The process is tedious, but if, O'Donnell did pass Weems the drive, it would explain why both men are dead. And raises some interesting possibilities."

"No." Reece had to force his balled hand to relax. "Gene O'Donnell wasn't in the game. He was simply doing me a favor."

"We've seen O'Donnell's impressive military service record and I admit it isn't likely, but that isn't to say Arthur Weems didn't take the flash drive without Mr. O'Donnell's knowledge or consent. He placed the drive in the front pocket of his jacket. A simple bump, nimble fingers…" He shrugged.

Reece was willing to concede that possibility.

"Weems followed him outside but dropped back. We haven't identified the person working with Weems. Mr. O'Donnell went straight to his truck. He answered his cell phone as he climbed inside. The call was from his foreman, Fred Vargas. It's been confirmed that a backhoe hired by the firm hit an underground gas line. Vargas called O'Donnell to report this. O'Donnell drove straight to the job site."

Yes, he would have, but Reece flinched as he realized what that meant. Smith nodded grimly.

"Exactly. An unknown number of people were on the scene when he arrived, including his crew, firemen and officials from the gas company. We're checking names, but anyone could have approached him in a crowd like that."

"And I'd bet none of them had anything to do with the missing drive."

Smith continued, unperturbed. "O'Donnell mentioned to Vargas that he had an errand to run as soon as they finished."

"Which implies he had the drive with him at that point."

"Or thought he did. Mr. O'Donnell was highly visible until the crew was dismissed and everyone else left. Afterward, according to Mr. Vargas, the two men stood outside the trailer talking for approximately forty-some minutes. O'Donnell went inside and Vargas drove straight home. He said no one else was left at the site."

"Because they were already inside the trailer."

"Possibly. Evidence indicates there had to be at least three people besides O'Donnell. Both bodies showed trauma evidence prior to the explosion and fire."

"Gene knew how to handle himself. It would have taken three men to bring him down."

"Mr. O'Donnell suffered a blunt-force injury to his head before the explosion and fire. The medical examiner indicates both men were alive, but most likely unconscious when the trailer blew up."

Reece swore long and hard.

"It is likely Mr. O'Donnell would have died of his wound, anyhow, without regaining consciousness."

"Weems, too?"

"No."

"So they deliberately killed him."

"Yes. Our British counterparts were surprised to learn we hadn't recovered the flash drive."

"What do the Brits have to do with this?"

"It seems you weren't the only agent making an attempt to acquire the information that night. British intelligence had their own man inside with the same objective. You simply got there first."

"Lucky me."

"That flash drive contains information about a planned attack we suspect is imminent, as well as a list of active cell members."

Reece whistled silently.

"We do not believe that Ms. O'Donnell knowingly has the flash drive. However, she is suddenly at the center of a great deal of attention. She needs our protection."

"You weren't interested before."

"Our mistake."

Reece felt a ball of ice settle in his gut. "You want to use her as bait."

Smith continued to regard him without expression. Only the flicker of his eyes told Reece he had the right of it.

"The answer is no."

"Someone believes she can lead them to the drive."

"She can't."

"Someone killed two civilians and risked the publicity of a police investigation in order to cover his identity."

"And you want to put her on a leash and dangle her out there for him to snatch."

"Isn't that what nearly happened last night?"

"What do you know about last night?"

He held up a palm. "Only what you told Mr. Ramsey."

"You've tapped into Mark's phone line?"

"Mr. Ramsey is exceptionally good at what he does. Fortunately, we have people who are better. I suspect Ms. O'Donnell will be more than willing to work with us to bring this situation to a close."

"Or what? You'll force her? I told her I work for the government."

His eyes narrowed.

"She isn't happy, but she was well on her way to figuring it out and my cover's blown, anyway. I've earned her trust and I'm not going to hang her out to dry."

"I said we'd protect her."

"I know exactly where your priorities lie."

"Then, you know we'll do what is necessary."

His gaze flicked to something behind Reece. He whirled. With an agent on either side, Kelly was being hustled across the parking lot toward a nondescript panel van.

Chapter Eleven

Reece ran toward Kelly, pulling his gun as he went.

"Kelly! Drop!"

Her head jerked up. Their eyes met. Kelly let her body go boneless, as she'd done last night. The men staggered. One let go. Reece brought up his weapon and fired. The bullet smashed through the windshield of the van. Someone screamed. Civilians began running. Kelly struggled against the hand still holding her.

"Let me go! Help! Someone help!"

He could have kissed her. Both agents drew their weapons.

"Police officer," Reece shouted. "Get down on the ground! Now!"

Reece didn't expect it to work and it didn't, but it did achieve the desired goal. There was more pandemonium. People in the parking lot continued taking cover. Kelly struggled free of the man who tried to haul her to her feet.

A young black male abruptly sprinted toward her from the other side. He carried a gun, as well. "Police! Let the woman go!"

The scene was turning into exactly the sort of utter chaos that the agents wanted to avoid. As if on command, they abandoned Kelly and sprinted for the van. The vehicle pulled out of the parking lot with a squeal of tires.

Reece tossed a look over his shoulder to find Smith. There was no sign of the other man.

"I'm Carey Johnson," the man announced as Reece reached them. "I work for Mark. I brought the Ferrari. Get her out of here before the cops arrive. I'll do what I can to stall them."

"Let him know his phones are bugged and you were probably tailed. Come on, Kelly."

She took his hand and they ran for the car. She started slowing when she didn't see the red Maserati. Reece indicated the silver Ferrari with the dark, tinted windows. Her eyes widened, but she didn't waste time on questions. She climbed in and was still reaching for her seat belt as he pulled out of the parking lot leaving startled people in his wake.

"They said they were government agents," she told him. "They had badges."

"I'm sure they did. They were."

Her mouth fell open. He deftly maneuvered through the now heavy Sunday morning traffic as if it were nonexistent. Had she picked up on Mark's name?

"You shot at them!"

"I shot at their car," he corrected.

"Are you insane?"

"It's a distinct possibility. I think it's safe to say I don't work for them, anymore."

She sank back against the soft leather seat. "I don't even know how to respond to that. What's going on, Reece?"

"At the moment, you could say we're fugitives." He barely squeezed the Ferrari between a panel truck and an SUV.

"Good lord," she whispered.

"What?"

"If you don't slow down we're going to be dead fugitives!"

Reece tossed her a grin. "Trust me. I drive a lot better than I shoot."

"I don't understand any of this," Kelly complained.

"It's complicated."

"I can do complicated. Try me. We've got until we're killed in a car crash for explanations."

Reece chuckled. "Actually, we don't. Turn off your cell phone."

"Why?"

"They can use it to triangulate on us."

"Okay, you're scaring me." But she obeyed.

"Now start explaining, Reece. When you told me to drop I thought they were the bad guys."

"No, but they wanted to use you as bait. Bait in our line of work frequently ends up dead so I chose not to cooperate. If I made the wrong choice for you, I can give you a number to call. They'll be happy to send their agents to pick you up again."

"Bait for what?"

"Whoever it was that tried to kidnap you last night." A police car in the lane ahead of them turned down a side street without paying them any notice. Reece breathed a sigh of relief and increased his speed. "We need a different car. This one's too conspicuous."

"You think?"

He grinned.

"Where did you get it?"

"I have a friend with connections."

She braced her hands on the dashboard as he tore through a busy intersection.

"I hope he's a good friend, because we're either going to wreck his little toy or get arrested."

She gasped as he switched lanes with inches to spare between cars.

"You're driving like a crazy person! This is not a race car!"

"Actually, Ferrari builds some of the best race cars in the world."

"Give me the gun. I'm going to shoot you."

He laughed again. "Will you marry me?"

"No! Are we really fugitives?"

He shrugged. "I fired a gun in a public place." He sped through another intersection as the caution light changed to red.

"Oh, God. You could have hurt someone."

"Nah, we had plenty of room." He glanced over at her. "Oh, you mean, the gun. That's why I aimed at their van. They needed to know I was armed and serious."

Her nails began tapping the dash. "I'm a reasonable person." She flinched as he sped around a panel truck. "And I think I'm taking this all quite well, don't you agree?"

He slotted her another quick glance. "You've done amazingly well."

"Yes, I have. I haven't given in to hysterics and I haven't pressed you for the answers I deserve. But I want to know what's going on."

"Let me give you the short version, for now. I need to concentrate on my driving. I recovered some information while I was in Italy. Due to complications, I had to pass that information to a courier who carried it to the U.S. for me. He passed it to another courier and things fell apart. The information went missing. We assumed the other side took it back. However, now it appears that wasn't the case and we don't know where the information is."

Kelly waited. When he didn't say more, she leaned forward. "That's it? That's all you're going to tell me?"

"I told you it was the short version."

She inhaled and clutched at her seat belt as they zipped around a car pulling out from a gas station and darted between a bus and a sedan full of elderly people. Reece knew he was taking crazy chances, but the more distance he put between them and the harbor, the better chance they had of not being stopped. It was several minutes before he realized that Kelly was entirely too silent.

"Kelly—"

"Was your missing information on a flash drive?"

Silently, he swore.

"James Prince said my father had a flash drive that belonged to him."

Startled, he nearly sideswiped a VW when he glanced over at her. He'd forgotten he'd asked her for the flash drive as James Prince, but she'd had no problem putting those two pieces of information together.

"Leah was wrong. He isn't a vampire, he's a spy. James Prince was the second courier, wasn't he?"

The curse slipped out as he raced to make a green light.

"It makes perfect sense. My father wasn't a spy, but he worked for a man who was. James Prince hid the flash drive in the trailer or he gave it to my father and asked him to hold on to it. Dad wouldn't have thought twice about doing the man a favor."

"Kelly—"

"That's why he was murdered. Someone took the flash drive, killed my dad and set it up to look like a drunken brawl and the police bought the whole package. James Prince is trying to get it back." Her voice rose with excitement and certainty. "That's why he got in touch with me. He agreed to help me so he could find where Dad hid the flash drive."

"Okay, this is not a good time to be having this conversation," Reece told her firmly. "I need to stay focused on the road. Traffic's picking up." And he didn't want to tell her the truth while he was careening down the busy streets.

"I'm right. I know I am. James Prince is involved! We find out who he really is and we get some answers. Think about it, Reece. How else would he know to ask about the flash drive? Dad never used a flash drive. He's still using zip drives. Was using zip drives." She shook her head at the slip. "It explains why Dad was killed and why someone broke into his apartment. Reece, it even explains that poor man who was killed outside *your* apartment. Whoever is looking for the drive was checking your apartment because you were hanging around me. That's how your cover got blown, isn't it?"

Reece clenched his jaw. There was no way to stop her. Her mind was racing, slotting what she knew into a working hypothesis.

"But you already knew all this." Her voice slowed with suspicion. "That's why you were outside the apartment that night, wasn't it? You were there to find the flash drive, too."

"Kelly, do you trust me?"

Her hesitation was all the answer he needed. "I *want* to trust you."

"Fair enough. I don't want to lie to you. And you have questions I can't answer."

"I'm right, aren't I?"

"That's one of those questions I can't answer."

"I thought you quit working for them."

"We need to find that flash drive."

Kelly studied his profile. His jaw was set, his expression forbidding. He might not want to work for his secret government organization, anymore, but he was still loyal. And he hadn't told her she was wrong, which was almost as good as admitting she was right.

James Prince had gotten her father killed. No wonder he wouldn't meet her face to face. No wonder he'd agreed to be her silent partner so easily, the bastard. Did he think he could assuage his guilt so easily?

That her father had been helping the government came as no surprise. Patriotism was as much a part of him as honesty and integrity. And, while she was furious with James Prince for involving him, strangely, at the same time, she was comforted by the thought that his death hadn't been meaningless. He had thwarted people who stood against every principal he believed in.

Moisture filled her eyes as tears clogged the back of her throat. She would not cry. Her father had done his part, now she needed to do hers. If he'd hidden the flash drive, she'd find it and get it where it needed to go.

"Aren't I bait, anyhow?"

"Not if I can help it."

His harsh tone surprised her while it warmed something cold inside her.

"One dead O'Donnell is more than enough. This isn't your problem."

"It was my father's. That makes it mine."

He flashed her an inscrutable look. Reece obviously wasn't going to answer any more questions so she fell silent as he steered the car with reckless speed through the bustling streets.

His hands rested on the steering wheel, the long tapered fingers curved about the wheel with easy confidence. Only hours before, they'd curved over her skin with that same effortless assurance.

She shook the thought aside. "Why did you make love with me?"

"I figured it would be more fun than playing cards." He shot her a quick glance. "Is this one of those relationship questions?"

"I haven't known you long enough to have a relationship question."

"Just long enough to spend the night making love with me, huh?"

She would not blush. "Whose side are you on, Reece?"

"Yours."

Her heart skipped a beat. "You barely know me."

"You're wrong, Kelly. I know all there is to know about you. I know you're beautiful inside and out. You're loyal. You're honest—"

"If you try to pet me I'll bite your hand off."

He grinned. "Right. No petting. Although, if done correctly, petting can be fun."

"Not in a car masquerading as a jet airplane on a busy highway."

"Good point."

"And stop trying to distract me."

"I like distracting you, Kelly."

"If we find the drive, will they arrest you?"

His smile was warm. "Worried about me?"

"Should I be?"

"No."

"So where do we start?"

Smith had Mark's phone line tapped, but Reece had told Mark he wouldn't take Kelly to her office. While it was still a risk, he figured that made it the safest place they could go for the moment. "I'm going to drop you off at Custom Concepts."

"You aren't dropping me anywhere, mister. Besides, that's the first place they'll look."

Reece shook his head. "As long as you stay away from the windows and don't answer the door or the telephone there's no reason for anyone to suspect you're there."

"And where do you think you'll be?"

"I have to see someone."

"Then, I'm going with you."

"You can't."

She glared at him. "Why not?"

"Because you'd look woefully out of place in a men's restroom."

"You're going to meet a man in a restroom." She infused the flat statement with disbelief.

Reece sighed. "I'm going to drive to the airport to search a men's restroom. Then, I'm going to call someone I'm hoping can help us. You can't go with me, but there's something you can do while you wait. Make a list of every person your father trusted with his life. Better yet, make a list of every person your father would have trusted with *your* life."

"Why?"

"Because he loved you, Kelly."

"How do you know?"

"I can hear that love every time you mention him."

She swallowed hard. Reece could be so maddening and then he'd say something like this. She shook her head against the distraction.

Reece's sigh was just the slightest breath of air. "Your dad is the person who went to the airport to meet the courier, Kelly. He was being watched. If he knew that and believed he was going to be picked up, what would he have done?"

"Made sure the drive was safe."

"Exactly."

"He wouldn't leave it in a men's room in a public airport," she protested.

"He might if he thought he had no choice."

"Why would he think that? Because of the person who was watching him?"

"There was undoubtedly more than one, Kelly. We've only identified one so far."

"Then, why don't you go question him? Or is that the person you're going to go see?"

Reece shook his head. "He's dead. He died in the fire and explosion with your father."

Shock rippled through her. "You know who the second victim was?"

"Arthur Weems. Does the name mean anything to you?"

"No." She took a minute to think and came up blank. "I've never heard of him. Should I have?"

"Not unless your father mentioned his name. You're sure he didn't?"

"Not that I recall. Who is he? Was he?" she amended quickly.

"Arthur Weems has been on our watch list for a couple of years now."

"He was an enemy agent?"

Reece shook his head. "We thought he might be a mole because of the company he's been seen keeping in England."

"He was British?"

"On his father's side. He had dual citizenship. His mother was American with ties to Pakistan."

"Oh."

"Yeah. He grew up mostly in Europe and Great Britain, but he attended college here in the United States."

"And you just let him run free?"

"He's never given us a reason to bring him in for questioning. But we keep an eye on people who have friends we don't like."

"Obviously not a close one or my father might

still be alive." She regretted the bite of her words as soon as she uttered them, but Reece didn't look offended, just the opposite, in fact.

"I can't argue with that."

"I'm sorry. I'm just feeling…"

"Frustrated? Know the feeling. Kelly, I'm not dumping you to get rid of you. It'll take me a couple of hours to run out to the airport, check out the restroom and head back."

"Dad wouldn't have left it there."

"Under normal circumstances, I'd agree, but we're running out of places to look. I don't like leaving you alone, but I really think you'll be safer at the warehouse than with me. They may be watching the airports. Please. Will you wait there for me?"

"Do I have a choice?"

He slanted her a serious look. "Always."

"What happens if I say no?"

"We'll figure out someplace else for you to stay. I thought at least at Custom Concepts you might have things you could do to stay occupied until I got back, but, if you'd prefer a motel room or something, say the word."

"You make it really hard to stay annoyed with you."

"Good."

"But I'm not happy about this."

"Neither am I. I'll hurry."

"Please don't. You may be working on a pilot's license, but roads are for driving, not flying, even if this car does sound like a jet plane."

His smile was boyishly impish. He insisted on driving her to the door even though Kelly pointed out that a Ferrari in her parking lot was going to attract a lot of notice if anyone was around.

Reece stopped her when she would have climbed out.

"Take my gun."

"No!"

His eyes held her gaze. "Take it."

"I wouldn't know what to do with it."

"Point and press."

"I could kill someone!"

"That's the point. Take it, Kelly."

Gingerly, she accepted the heavy metal.

"This is the safety. Flick this to turn it off. And don't use the phones. I can't be sure they aren't bugged."

"I hate this."

"I'm sorry." He cupped her face. The kiss was so tender she could have cried. "I'll be back as soon as I can."

"You'd better be."

Kelly shoved the heavy gun in the pocket of her jacket and hoped the seams would hold. She let herself inside the building without looking back.

Pellonia came running full tilt down the shadowy hallway at the sound of the engine roaring to life.

"Hey there, cat. It's good to see you, too. Now we've both been abandoned here. Well, not completely. There's always my dad's truck or one of the company trucks if we want to run away."

She walked back to her desk with the cat scampering at her heels. The minute she sat down, Pellonia jumped into her lap and settled with a satisfied purr. Kelly found much of her tension easing as she stroked the soft fur.

"So, tell me, did you find any mice in your prowling last night?"

Pellonia raised her chin for a light scratch. Kelly thought about taking off her jacket, but there was a chill in the air so she kept it on and pulled out a pad of paper to list the people her father had considered friends. Time crawled. Putting on some coffee, she turned her attention to the inevitable paperwork generated by Custom Concepts. It kept her from pacing, even if her heart wasn't in it.

She wanted to call Leah and explain what had happened. Knowing her friend, Leah had probably tried to call her all afternoon. She'd be worried. Besides, Kelly wanted to know if Heath and Rebecca had Leah's coat. She also wanted to call Mark Ramsey and have him start an investigation on Curtis Long.

Reece had paid little attention to her suggestion that Curtis Long and James Prince were the same man, but he'd have to pay attention now, because James Prince headed her list of people her father trusted. Eugene O'Donnell hadn't spoken of James Prince often, but, when he had, there'd been no doubt that he liked the other man a great deal.

Her dad was an excellent judge of character, however, it was possible James Prince had fooled even him. She really needed to talk to Mark Ramsey and see if he'd learned anything yet.

Something tickled the back of her mind. She couldn't quite decide what it was, but she knew it had to do with Mark Ramsey. Something someone had said. Her fingers drummed the desktop.

I'm Carey Johnson. I work for Mark.

Kelly tensed. The man at the marina had told Reece that when he'd come running over holding a gun. Reece hadn't been surprised.

Let him know his phone lines are bugged.

She drew in a ragged breath.

I work for Mark.

Coincidence. It had to be a coincidence. Mark was a common name. There must be countless numbers of men named Mark in the D.C. area alone. But her heart began beating faster, all the same.

She trusted Reece.

Didn't she?

Pellonia looked up from the corner of her desk and mewed softly.

"Can we trust him, cat?"

She did trust Reece. "I'm not going down that road," she told the cat.

Reece had fought to save her last night. More important, he'd shown her in countless small ways that he cared. She stroked Pellonia's head and was rewarded with a low, rumbly purr.

"It wasn't just sex, cat. I trust myself to know the difference. I'm falling in love with him." The animal blinked and butted its head against her hand. "I know, I know. I've only known him a matter of days. Foolish of me, but there it is."

I work for Mark.

Kelly tensed against the disquiet of those words.

"Even if it's the same Mark, so what? Reece uses the same lawyer as James Prince because the man is tops in his field. The same probably applies to Ramsey Inc."

Hadn't she called Mark Ramsey because his was the company that provided security to the warehouse complex? Except, why hadn't Reece said anything when she'd told him she called Mark Ramsey?

"There's no reason to start feeling paranoid, cat."

Except that someone really was after her.

If her father had had this mysterious flash drive,

where would he have hidden it? The trailer was the most likely place, but that had burned to the ground. The apartment? Someone had already searched it.

But how thoroughly? She'd never known a man yet who could find something he'd been sent to look for.

She needed to look for herself. Only, Reece had told her to wait. How long had she been sitting here? Was there time for her to run over to the apartment and get back before Reece did? Would it be safe?

Her gaze fell on the wall of pictures opposite her desk. She stopped stroking Pellonia and stood. Crossing to the wall, she stared hard at the center picture of her dad.

"You wouldn't hide something like that at a busy airport, would you, Dad? Something that important, you would have wanted to get where it belonged right away. If you thought you were in danger, you'd go to the nearest cop for help, wouldn't you? But you didn't. You went to the site because of an immediate problem."

Her father's smiling face seemed to be looking right at her, filled with pride. She reached out to trace the photo with her finger and stopped. Eyes narrowed, she stared closely at the image. Her heart began thumping wildly.

It wasn't possible.

Was it?

She tried to lift the Plexiglas box frame from the wall. It wouldn't budge. The thumping grew stronger. Who nailed picture frames to the wall?

She began to work the box off the white cardboard frame only to find the cardboard had been reinforced with wood. The wood was attached to the wall. As the Plexiglas and cardboard came free of the wood, the picture slid to the floor unnoticed. Panic clawed at her insides. Kelly stared at the pinhole camera eye that was clearly exposed.

Chapter Twelve

Adrenaline coursed through her. Kelly tossed the plastic frame on her desk, startling the cat. There was no telling how much time she had. She scooped Pellonia from the floor, snatched up her purse and keys and ran down the hall to the front door. The cat squirmed to get down, but she managed to hold on as she unlocked the door, relocked it and ran to her dad's truck.

Dropping Pellonia onto the backseat, she started the engine. Reece had been wrong. Custom Concepts was anything but safe. His fellow agents knew exactly where she was.

Pellonia mewed unhappily and slid across the seat as Kelly rocketed out of the parking lot. "Sorry, cat. I'm not as good at this as Reece is." And her dad's old pickup truck was no sports car. Driving like a maniac was only likely to cause her to wreck, so she slowed down as soon as she reached the main road. The question was, where to go?

The apartment and Leah's were out. She could go back to the boat, but that didn't seem like a good idea, either.

Rebecca! No one would think to look for her there and Rebecca could call Heath. As Reece's friend, she was pretty sure Heath would help if he could.

Pellonia startled her by jumping onto the passenger seat.

"Okay. Just don't get under my feet while I'm driving. I should have thought to grab your carrier. I hope Rebecca likes cats."

She drove impatiently until she hit a red traffic light. Finally she was able to dig through her purse and find the business cards the other woman had given her. One was her personal card while the second was for her business office. The personal card had an address in downtown Washington, not far from the Bethesda line.

Parking proved to be a problem, but eventually Kelly lucked out, finding a place on the street only a block away. That still left her with the problem of Pellonia. She didn't want to leave the animal in the truck, but, without something to carry her in, there was no choice. She couldn't risk the animal getting loose and running out into traffic.

The temperature was only in the fifties, so the truck wasn't likely to get too hot. Cracking both windows to get a little airflow, she eyed the cat, who had curled on the passenger seat for a nap.

"Okay, wait here, guard the truck and stay out of trouble. I'll be back as soon as I can."

If Rebecca wasn't home, Kelly didn't know what she was going to do. Fortunately, the other woman answered the buzzer after only a short delay.

"Rebecca, it's Kelly O'Donnell. I'm really sorry. I know this is a huge imposition, but I need a favor."

"Kelly? Come on up."

She reached for the handle the moment the buzzer released the lock and it wasn't until she stepped in the elevator that it occurred to her she might be putting Rebecca in danger. A bit late to worry about that now. She found Rebecca waiting in the hall when the doors opened.

Rebecca was dressed casually in jeans and a sweatshirt. Her long dark hair was piled on top of her head and the scent of disinfectant clung to her clothes.

"Hi!"

"Rebecca, I'm sorry to barge in on you like this."

"No problem. I was scrubbing floors and doing laundry. Trust me, you're a welcome reprieve. And I'm glad to see you're okay. The way you and Reece disappeared last night, we thought something was wrong."

"It was. A man tried to kidnap me."

Rebecca gaped. "Are you okay?"

"Yes. Reece chased him off."

"Let's go inside and you can tell me about it." Kelly followed her down the hall, grateful for the other woman's relaxed manner. It helped with her own tension.

"I have to warn you, Rebecca. I'm in a mess so if you don't want to get involved, feel free to say so."

"Define mess," Rebecca requested as she opened the door to her apartment and ushered Kelly inside.

"Government agents, missing information, dead people. You know, Washington at its finest."

"Oh, well, then, no problem."

Only slightly relieved, Kelly returned her smile, wondering how Rebecca would feel when she learned Kelly was serious. The apartment was bright and cheerful with lots of neutral colors and splashes of reds and pale yellow.

"This is nice."

"Thanks. Would you like something to drink? I've got iced tea and water and not a whole lot more since I haven't been to the store yet."

"No, I'm fine. Thanks."

"Okay, pull up a chair and tell me how I can help."

"I need to get hold of Heath. I'm hoping he can help me locate Reece."

"Reece is missing?"

"Not exactly. I was supposed to wait for him at

the warehouse, but I discovered a hidden camera in my office. I don't know who it belongs to, but I decided not to hang around and wait to find out."

"A hidden camera? Kelly, this is serious. You need to call the police. Someone's stalking you. You said he even tried to kidnap you."

"It's more complicated than that. Apparently, my dad was a government courier. It appears that he was killed by someone who wanted what he was carrying!"

"Kelly!"

She ignored the woman's shocked expression. "The information went missing and it appears his killer thinks I can help him find it." She shook her head. "I can't."

"You need to call the police right now. Or maybe the state department."

"I can't explain, but I need to get ahold of Reece first."

Rebecca nodded. "I'm sure Heath has his phone number. They live in the same building, you know."

"No. I didn't know."

Rebecca shot her a puzzled glance.

"I don't know all that much about Reece," Kelly admitted. And just how much she didn't know was being pounded home with the force of a sledgehammer. "The thing is, I don't need his phone number, because he won't answer. He turned off his cell phone and told me not to use mine. Apparently, they can triangulate on the cell phones to find a person's location."

"Are we talking terrorists here or what?"

Kelly sighed. "I don't know. Maybe. All I know is someone tried to kidnap me last night and again this morning. Everyone wants the flash drive my dad was supposed to have."

"Okay, I'm thinking we should call the FBI."

She shook her head. It would be so much easier if she could tell Rebecca that Reece worked for the government, but she didn't think he'd appreciate that.

"I can't call anyone. Look, I know how this sounds, but there are things I can't tell you. I just need to reach Reece before he goes to the warehouse and walks into a trap." She started to rise. "Coming here was a bad idea. I'm sorry, Rebecca. I shouldn't have."

Rebecca laid a hand on her arm. "You're here now. Let me help."

"You can't."

"You wanted me to call Heath," she prompted.

"Because I had the insane notion that somehow he could help me figure out a way to leave a message for Reece."

"It's not insane. As I said, they live in the same building. Is Reece apt to go home? Heath could slip a note under the door."

Kelly considered that. Reece would be frantic

when he found out she was missing—if he wasn't killed when he went to Custom Concepts to get her.

"You're taking this awfully calmly," she stalled, trying to think.

"Yes, well, my insides are in knots if it's any consolation, but I can see you're really upset. I have a spare bedroom. You can hide at my place for a few days."

"No. The people who are after this flash drive are serious. They've already killed four people."

Rebecca blinked. "Are we talking about that photographer who was killed outside your apartment building?"

"And the security guard in Reece's building," Kelly confirmed. "Reece thinks the security guard was trying to stop someone from breaking into his apartment."

"Why would someone break into Reece's apartment? Never mind," she amended at whatever she saw on Kelly's face. "I didn't realize you and Reece were so…close."

"We aren't." She could feel her skin heating. "I mean, we are sort of, but it's complicated." She changed the subject quickly. "I like your idea of leaving Reece a note under his door. If you could call Heath for me…"

Rebecca lifted the telephone and began to dial. Kelly noticed she didn't have to look up his number, but Heath wasn't home and he wasn't answering his cell phone. Rebecca left messages on both asking him to call her back.

"I didn't use your name to be safe," she told Kelly, setting the phone down.

"I appreciate that."

"Listen, my stomach's grumbling and I've got zip to offer you for lunch. Why don't we run over to the café down the street and grab something? I'll take my cell phone in case Heath calls us back."

Kelly hesitated. "I've got a cat out in my truck."

"As in four legs, whiskers and a tail?"

She smiled. "Yes."

"Bring it in."

Kelly eyed the cream-colored suede sofa and shook her head. "She's got claws and I'm not sure how housebroken she is. She's a stray I've been feeding. I couldn't go home after the photographer was murdered so Reece rescued her for me."

Rebecca's eyebrows arched. Kelly knew she was blushing again. "I wouldn't want her to scratch your furniture."

"We could always put her in the back bedroom."

"I can't stay, Rebecca. It isn't safe."

"What about lunch? You have to eat and no one will think to look for you here."

That was true enough. "Let me check on Pellonia first."

"Pellonia?"

"Reece named her after some goddess."

"Uh-huh." Rebecca grinned. "Better be careful, friend, when a guy starts naming your cats—"

"Rebecca!" But she found herself smiling back. "Okay, he's…special. And maybe if we find the drive and don't get killed there will be time to find out how special. In the meantime, if Pellonia isn't stressing out, I'd be happy to go to lunch with you."

"Give me a minute to change."

Kelly walked to the window while Rebecca changed into a light pink blouse and dark slacks. Outside, the street was busy with people moving briskly along the sidewalk. She could just see the truck from here and, as far as she could tell, no one seemed the least bit interested in it. She really hoped coming here hadn't been a mistake.

They left the building a few minutes later. Kelly stayed alert, but no one approached. When they reached the truck she found Pellonia still curled on the front seat asleep.

"I guess she'll be okay for a little while."

"Good. The café's on the next block."

The small bakery café was doing a brisk luncheon trade, but they lucked out and snagged a booth. Over lunch, they discussed possible hiding places for the flash drive.

"What about your dad's truck?"

"I don't think so." Kelly swallowed the last bite of her sandwich, amazed to realize she'd eaten everything on her plate. "Dad never locks the truck and I'm sure the people who searched his apartment searched it, too. Still, it might be worth looking in the tool case bolted to the bed. That's always locked and a flash drive is small enough to be overlooked if the person searching was in a hurry."

She frowned, trying to picture her dad hiding it somewhere. "If I could just go back to the apartment. I'll bet it's there and they missed it."

Rebecca's eyes gleamed. "Why don't we? These people can't be everywhere, and you said they don't really want you, just the flash drive. We should be safe enough."

"We?"

She smiled. "I'm willing to help."

"I can't ask you to do that."

"You didn't, I volunteered. It's broad daylight on a Sunday afternoon. No one's going to start trouble with a lot of witnesses around."

"Ha. You don't know Reece," Kelly told her.

"What?"

"Never mind. What about Heath?"

"When he calls, we'll tell him where we are."

Rebecca's enthusiasm was contagious. Kelly was tired of sitting around letting things happen. If she found the flash drive, this whole nightmare might end.

"Let's do it."

Before they could call for the check, Rebecca's cell phone rang. "It's Heath," she told Kelly. "Hi there, thanks for calling me back. I have Kelly here with me and she's in a bit of bind. What? No. Reece is running errands somewhere. Kelly says his cell phone is turned off. Uh-huh. We're just down the street finishing lunch."

Her expression changed. She glanced at Kelly nervously.

"Why not? What's going on, Heath? Yes, okay. Twenty minutes? Where are you? Okay. We'll wait."

Kelly knew her expression mirrored the racing of her heart. "What's wrong?"

"I don't have a clue." She closed the cell phone and placed it back in her purse. "Heath said not to go back to my apartment. He sounded very intense."

"Maybe Reece talked to him."

Rebecca shook her head. "I don't think so. He wanted to know how to reach Reece. He wants us to give him twenty minutes and he'll pick us up."

"He wants us to wait here?"

She nodded. "You aren't dieting, are you?"

Kelly followed her gaze to a passing waiter bearing a sinfully loaded tray of desserts. Her nerves were jumping, but she managed a weak smile. "Only on occasions that don't involve dessert."

Rebecca returned her smile with a shaky one of her own. "I knew I liked you."

DISAPPOINTMENT WEIGHED HEAVILY as Reece left the men's room after a fruitless search. He'd been so sure Gene had hidden the drive in there.

Maybe Smith was right. Maybe Arthur Weems had lifted it without Gene being aware that it had been taken. About to exit the terminal, he stopped at the sight of a familiar face. Oliver Kendall stood off to one side watching the ticket counter intently.

"Oliver?"

Oliver sent a distracted glance in his direction. Annoyance was immediately replaced by surprise when he recognized Reece. "Hey, man, what are you doing here?"

"I was going to ask you the same thing."

"I dropped off a friend of Heath's." He nodded in the direction of the busy counter.

Reece followed the nod and his chest tightened. A young man with his arm in a sling was checking in at the counter.

"Did you say a friend of Heath's?"

"Yeah, why? Do you know him?"

"We weren't formally introduced," he told him wryly, remembering the man with the knife outside Kelly's apartment. There was nothing to say this man and his opponent were one and the same except for a prickle he couldn't ignore.

"Yeah," Oliver acknowledged. "That was a real mob the Brits invited the other night."

Reece eyed him sharply. "He was at the party in McLean?"

"Sure, along with half the city. You and your date split awfully sudden after the lights went out. Afraid of the dark?"

"Looking for a bit of privacy."

Oliver winked knowingly. "Can't say I blame you. Kelly's an attractive package. What brings you here?"

"Searching for a missing bit of luggage." Reece studied Heath's friend. The build was right and he moved with a similar fluid assurance as he took his ticket and strode off down the concourse without a backward glance.

"Not very friendly, is he?"

Oliver shrugged. "Kelvin's running late. He'll be lucky to make it through security and get to his gate, as it is."

"Kelvin what?"

"Huh? Oh. Tisler. Kelvin Tisler."

"He's going back to England?"

"Flight 6109. You want to grab some lunch?"

"Another time. I'm also running late."

"Going to see Kelly?"

Reece swung his gaze back to Oliver. "Why?"

"Because, if you aren't, I'd like to give her a call myself."

"Forget it," he told him, annoyed by the gleam of interest in Oliver's eyes. "The lady's taken. Permanently."

"Sounds serious."

"I'll send you an invitation to the wedding. Catch you later."

Reece left the stunned man standing there and headed briskly for the parking garage. His thoughts were spinning and their direction made him ill. He liked Heath. He trusted him, but he didn't trust coincidence.

Kelvin Tisler could have broken his arm in a number of ways besides the knife fight with Reece, but Heath had insisted Reece attend last night's party. And he was the one who'd sent Kelly to the hall to wait.

Reece didn't want to believe that Heath had set her up, but Heath had been at the party in Italy, as well, and, somehow, he'd known when Reece had been arrested. They'd stayed in the same hotel. Heath had been in and out of Reece's room several times. He'd had potential access to Reece's passport. And there was no getting around the fact that the coincidences surrounding Heath were mounting.

A restless urgency grew inside him. Reece tapped

his fingers against the steering wheel as he waited to pay his toll and leave the parking garage. He couldn't even call Kelly because he'd told her not to use the phone.

He ground his teeth in frustration. Finally, he was on the highway, moving with purpose. Mark's phone lines were tapped, but Reece had his private cell-phone number. He'd have to chance using his own cell phone rather than waste time looking for a pay phone.

Mark answered right before the call would have switched to the answering system.

"Turn off your cell phone and meet me where we transferred the Lamborghini in an hour," he told Mark the moment he heard him say hello.

"Are you coming in hot?" Mark demanded after a beat.

Reassured, Reece relaxed a fraction. "No, but you might."

"I'll watch for outriders. Kelly found a camera and took off."

Reece swore. Fear for her mixed with a host of recriminations. "Make it forty minutes."

He disconnected and turned off the phone. He should have told Kelly the truth from the start. Now she was out there alone and he had no idea who she might have turned to for help. He didn't think she'd risk bringing Leah into this situation, but, with a pang, he realized he didn't know any of Kelly's other friends.

And he wanted to know. He wanted to know everything about her. She could be anywhere. And, if she trusted the wrong person, she could be dead.

THEY WERE STILL SITTING over glasses of iced tea in their now isolated booth when Heath walked up and slid in beside Rebecca. "What's going on, Heath?" she asked.

"Reece and Kelly are in a spot of trouble."

She made a face. "We know that. That's why we called you."

"This isn't the best place to talk." He reached for his wallet and pulled out several bills. Setting them on top of the check sitting on the table, he stood. "We'll go to my flat."

Uneasy and not sure why, Kelly slid out and stood. Her unease grew as Heath hustled them onto the sidewalk and set off at a brisk walk.

"Have you talked to Reece?" Kelly asked, deliberately slowing her pace as they approached a dark blue BMW. Heath opened the doors. Rebecca took the passenger seat, looking nervous, as well.

"No. Get in, Kelly."

"I left the cat in Dad's truck."

Heath frowned. "We'll stop and get her. Do you know where Reece is?"

Reluctantly, she settled on the buttery soft leather. "He mentioned the airport, but he didn't say which one."

Heath's frown deepened. Closing the doors, he walked around to the driver's side. As soon as he climbed in, he turned to look at her. "Why did he go to the airport?"

"He's looking for something."

For a long second he stared past her, lost in thought. "Don't tell me he thinks your father hid the flash drive at the airport?"

Prickles of alarm rose along her arms. "How do you know about my dad and the flash drive?"

He grimaced. "That will take some explaining and it can wait until we get to my place." He settled into place and started the engine.

It was possible Reece had told Heath about the situation, but unlikely. Kelly had a sinking feeling that she'd just made a serious mistake.

"I don't think so."

She fumbled the heavy gun from her coat pocket and pointed at him.

Rebecca inhaled sharply. Her eyes went wide.

Heath met her gaze in the rearview mirror. "You Yanks and your bloody guns."

"Sorry, but right now I have no reason to trust you or anyone else."

"No," he agreed slowly, "I don't suppose you do."

"Kelly, what are you doing?" Rebecca whispered.

"I'm tired of being jerked around. I want a simple answer. How do you know about the flash drive and my father?"

Heath's jaw clenched. He glanced at Rebecca and back at Kelly with a deep scowl. "Because I work for the Crown. The English government," he amended.

The gun began to waver as her hand shook. "You're a spy, too?"

The scowl became a grimace.

"A spy?" Rebecca's eyes darted from one to the other.

"Simple answer? Yes."

"You mean, like James Bond?" Rebecca demanded.

Kelly gripped the gun with both hands to keep it still. "I suppose you can prove that?"

"Actually, no. Not to *your* satisfaction, at any rate."

"Kelly, what's going on?"

"That's what I'm trying to figure out," she replied, without taking her eyes from Heath.

"I understand your misgivings," he told her. "This isn't going down a treat for me, either. But you have to trust me. I've known Reece, for years."

"Reece is a spy, too?" Rebecca demanded.

"So he says," Kelly agreed.

"He works for one of your many government organizations," Heath confirmed. "At least, according to my people."

"I don't believe this," Rebecca sputtered. "Is everyone I know a spy except me?"

Heath shrugged. "It isn't like the flicks depict. At least not most of the time," he amended ruefully, but his gaze remained on Kelly. "We weren't aware that your people knew about the information. Reece appropriated it from the computer that night before I could have a go. I was dangling from a balcony when all hell broke loose. I barely made it back inside before their people saw me."

Heath sounded so disgusted it was hard to doubt him. "Does Reece know about you?"

"No, and it's a bit of irony, that. Despite years of friendship, neither of us had a clue about the other. We should have suspected, I suppose, but there it is. I only learned of his role when I was asked to lend a hand getting him free in Italy. It was a right bit of a shocker, I can tell you."

"Getting him free from what?"

"The man who hosted the party that night is working with the terrorists. I'm not sure why, but he had some reason to suspect Reece stole the information from him. As he pretty much owned the town, it was no chore to set up a phony charge so the local constabulary would hold Reece while they searched for the information. Being as our governments are allies, I was asked to lend a hand when it appeared the arrest might stick out of spite."

"But you didn't tell him who you worked for?"

"No need, don't you see."

Rebecca eyed him narrowly. "No. I don't see. I thought you were old English money."

"My heritage is exactly as stated, I assure you. But in my country, even royalty is subject to military service. I simply continued on."

The words tripped off his lips so easily. Kelly wanted to accept them at face value, but caution wouldn't let her. He seemed relatively relaxed, but she wasn't all that good at reading body language.

"Why didn't you want us to go back to Rebecca's?"

"I am trying to protect both of you. You may have been followed there."

"And, let me guess, you want to use me as bait, too."

His gaze locked with hers. "As tempting as that might be, I suspect Reece would take serious umbrage. I don't fancy him having a go at me. But, if you aren't going to shoot me, I'd appreciate it if you'd at least put the safety back on before your weapon goes off. I'd hate to become a casualty due to a bloody pothole."

"Turn off the engine."

Heath hesitated, then did as she ordered. Kelly lowered the gun and put the safety back on. He'd sounded so disgusted she found it hard to doubt him. "Does Reece know about you?"

"No. We've been chums for years and neither of us had a clue."

"Why didn't you tell him?"

"That isn't how it works, Kelly. I'd have helped him free out of friendship, anyway."

"Are you going to tell Reece you're a spy?"

"Yes."

"What makes you think he'll believe you?"

He shrugged. "He'll believe me."

Despite the certainty in his voice, Kelly wasn't sure *she* could believe him.

"Is Curtis Long a spy, too?"

That brought sudden speculation to Heath's eyes as he contemplated her. "Funny you should mention him. I don't know." He spoke slowly, obviously thinking it through. "My impression was that Reece had simply used him to carry the flash drive into the States."

"Curtis Long is the person my dad met at the airport?"

Heath nodded cautiously. Rebecca watched them both intently, but Kelly barely spared her any notice. Her mind whirled, snapping bits and pieces together.

"So the security tapes at the airport show Curtis Long handing a flash drive to my father. And no one has seen it since."

"That's my understanding."

"Why does everyone assume the flash drive Curtis Long handed my father was the same one Reece gave him?"

Chapter Thirteen

Tooey's Garage was closed on Sundays, but a bright yellow Lotus was parked sideways in front of the bay doors. Mark leaned against the driver's side, ankles crossed, a pair of dark aviator glasses covering his eyes. He looked deceptively relaxed as Reece pulled up beside him.

"Impressive time. You should drive race cars."

Reece didn't smile back as he came around the car. "My mother objected. What happened?"

Mark straightened. "Kelly spotted the camera lens in her office, grabbed the cat and split in her dad's truck."

Reece gritted his teeth. "Tell me you had it tagged."

"Of course. The truck's in D.C. She isn't in it."

His insides twisted.

"There are a number of apartment buildings nearby. She could be in any one of them. Here's the address." Mark handed him an envelope. "I've got an operative watching. Reece, she's looked at that picture any number of times," he continued with a shake of his head, "I don't know what tipped her this time."

"This time she was paying attention. If she calls and asks, tell her the truth."

"Which truth?"

"James Prince has the warehouse wired. She thinks Curtis Long is James Prince."

"You going to tell her different?"

Reece grimaced. "Eventually."

"Your funeral. Directions and keys to a house in Arlington are also in the envelope. The place belongs to friends of mine. My firm monitors their security system." He fished a set of car keys from his pocket. "I'll swap you for the Lotus."

Reece eyed the bright yellow car. "Aviator glasses come as part of the package?"

Mark grinned. "Sorry, I didn't have a lot of color choices. They won't know this one."

"That's for sure. Smith's going to come knocking on your door."

"Figured as much. I'm on vacation."

"That won't hold him for long."

"Are you going to need long?"

Reece ran a hand through his hair. "I hope not."

Mark produced a cell phone from another pocket. "Keep in touch."

"Yours?"

"Not officially." He smiled. "What else do you need?"

"Kelly."

The smile turned rueful. "I wish you luck. She's got you on the ropes, pal."

"Want to come to the wedding?"

Mark whistled. "Counting chickens, aren't you?"

"That's the only thing keeping me sane at the moment." He clapped Mark on the back, handed him the keys to the Ferrari and climbed into the bright yellow Lotus. "Keep your head down."

"You do the same."

THE BATTERED OLD PICKUP was right where Mark had indicated. No sign of Kelly and nothing to tell Reece where she might have gone. Pellonia was curled up on the seat, asleep. Kelly must be nearby. She wouldn't abandon the cat, so likely, she had a friend in one of the buildings and would return soon. Unfortunately, there was no way to tell which building she was in.

Smith might know. He had access to more information than Reece and that could prove to be a problem. Reece needed to get to Kelly first.

There was no reason for her to connect the camera with him, therefore he could assume she would try to get a message to him. He didn't think she'd go back to the Haverdocks and that left—

Fear twisted inside him. He tamped it down while his mind raced. Heath had an unlisted phone number, but Rebecca had given Kelly her card.

Reaching for the cell phone, he called Mark.

"I need an address for Rebecca Holliman in D.C.," he told him without preamble.

"Hold on while I check."

Reece heard him tapping computer keys.

"On the money," Mark told him. The address he recited was one of the nearby buildings. "Here's the phone number."

Reece disconnected with thanks and dialed. An answering machine picked up. There were any number of reasons she might not answer, but if he guessed wrong, Kelly might die.

"YOU THINK CURTIS switched the flash drives?" Heath demanded.

Shoving the gun back in her jacket, Kelly climbed out of the car. "I have no idea, but it's something to think about." Then she was running down the street toward her father's truck. She expected Heath to come after her, but he didn't. She reached the truck unmolested and slid inside.

Pellonia was on the floor on the passenger side, playing with something.

"Stay out from under my feet, cat."

Kelly started the engine and pulled into traffic.

She had no clue where to go next. Involving one of her friends was out of the question. She didn't feel safe going back to the Haverdocks or the boat. That same logic eliminated her aunt and uncle's house, too. And, if they could trace her cell phone, they could undoubtedly trace her credit card and she didn't have much cash on her, making a motel problematic, as well.

She turned onto Canal Road with no destination in mind and tried to decide what Reece would do once he discovered her missing. The obvious starting point was Leah. If Kelly could leave her friend a message, Reece would get it eventually. If she kept the call short and turned the cell phone off afterward, a brief call seemed like an acceptable risk.

The parking lot along the canal was full. She double parked behind a pair of cars and left the engine running. Pellonia tossed her toy into the air and pounced. Jumping onto the seat, she dropped the item and looked at Kelly.

"What have you got, cat?"

Heart in her throat, she lifted her dad's wedding band. Pellonia batted at her hand, trying to take back the ring. Kelly ignored the cat. Until this moment, she hadn't given her dad's ring any thought. If she had, she would have assumed he was wearing it when he'd been murdered. But he always removed his ring when he was working and put it back on after he finished for the day. He had a habit of shoving it into his jacket pocket or his pants pocket if he wasn't wearing a jacket. But he always kept it on him. He said it brought him good luck.

Her fist closed over the ring. A terrible pang of grief cut through her. Pellonia apparently decided Kelly wasn't going to return the toy and was busy sticking her paw in the crevice between the seat.

"What are you doing, cat?"

Gently, Kelly pushed the animal aside and slid her fingers inside. An open package of gum and a loose key came free. There was no telling what the key belonged with. Pellonia batted at her hand, then went back to clawing the scuffed cloth seat.

Setting the ring and the key next to the gum, she slid her fingers between the two halves of the seat once more. Wedge tightly in the corner, she touched something smooth and plastic.

Her breath caught. Abruptly, she was panting, digging as furiously as Pellonia had done. Her dad tossed his jacket on the seat when he got too warm. Things frequently fell out of his pockets.

Kelly worked to free the plastic. She held the small item in her fingers in disbelief. And someone rapped on the driver's-side window.

"Hey, lady, you want to move so I can get out?"

She stared at the man without comprehension.

His expression changed from annoyance to concern.

"You okay, lady?"

Kelly managed a nod. "I'll move."

Heart racing, still gripping the flash drive, she put the truck in gear, driving automatically while chaos ruled her thoughts. Who should she call? The state department? The FBI? The CIA? The only one she wanted to call was Reece.

"Good guy or bad guy, cat?"

Pellonia ignored her to play with the ring. A bad guy wouldn't have bothered to rescue a stray cat.

"Okay. Let's get this to the state department and let them decide where it goes. Now, how do I get there from here?" She wasn't even sure where the building was located.

As she exited Canal Road, she glimpsed a bright yellow sports car zip around three cars on the double yellow line, closing the distance between them as if it were on a speedway and every second counted. Impossible, of course, but she only knew one person who drove like that.

The car zoomed around her dad's truck and braked hard as it came to a red traffic light.

Kelly didn't even blink when Reece leaped out of the yellow car and ran up to her window. "What are you doing here?" she demanded before he could say a word. "How did you know—"

"Follow me." He ran back to the sports car as the light turned to green.

Reece crossed the Chain Bridge, but bypassed the Parkway. He drove until he came to a strip mall. Kelly pulled up beside him when he parked well away from other cars. She shoved the flash drive into her pocket as he came over to the truck and opened her door.

"Grab the cat and get in the car. We'll come back for the truck later."

"You had one of those tracer things on my dad's truck! And how many sports cars do you own?"

"One. The Lamborghini. The others are borrowed."

"Did you know your friend Heath claims to be a spy, too?"

Reece stiffened. "When did you talk to Heath?"

"I just left him. He also wanted to take me for a ride."

Reece swore. "Kelly, get out. There may be more than one tracer on your dad's truck."

"Then this parking lot may get crowded. Seems to me, half of D.C. is interested in where I go. But there's no rush. As Rebecca pointed out, they don't want to shoot me. They only want to use me to get the flash drive."

"I don't want to use you, Kelly."

She wanted to believe him. Grabbing Pellonia and the ring she stepped out of the truck. Reece took the cat and hurried to the little yellow car.

"I found the flash drive," she told him as she sat down and he handed her Pellonia.

"What?"

"Close the door before she gets loose."

Reece closed the door and came around to the driver's side. "What do you mean, you found the flash drive?"

"Technically, Pellonia found it. It was caught in the seat of the truck." Reaching into her pocket she showed him.

His expression was stunned. "Put it away. It was there all this time?"

"Along with Dad's wedding ring." She held that up, as well. Pellonia immediately began batting at it. "You can't play with it here, cat. There's no room. What do your friends have against sedans, anyway?"

"One friend, and he knows I like fast cars."

"And fast women?"

Reece leaned over and kissed her. Pellonia swatted at him until he sat back. "Sorry, Pellonia," he apologized with a grin. He started the engine. "Marry me."

Her stomach quivered. "Not funny."

"It wasn't meant to be."

"You can't be serious."

"Never more so."

She stared at his handsome profile and realized she was trembling. "No."

"Why not?"

"For one thing, you're rich."

The corners of his lips edged upward. "Most women would consider that on the plus side."

"I am not most women."

"No, you certainly aren't. Is it my reputation?"

"Why are we having this conversation?"

He stopped for a traffic light and turned to face her. "I love you, Kelly."

"You don't even know me!"

His hand cupped her face lightly. "You've got it wrong. *You* don't know *me*." Traffic began to move. He dropped his hand to face forward again. "But I'm willing to give you time to rectify that."

Kelly couldn't stop staring at him. He reached over and captured her hand. "It'll all work out."

"Sure. An internationally famous playboy who just happens to be a real life James Bond wants to marry me. What's not to work out?"

He flashed her a heart-stopping grin. "Exactly."

"I must be dreaming."

"As long as you don't consider it a nightmare."

She stared at the passing scenery, her stomach fluttering. He actually thought he wanted to marry her. And she had the craziest impulse to say yes. "Where are we going?"

He squeezed her hand and released it. "My place. It's closest and we need to call Smith right away.

Once the word gets out that his people have the drive our troubles are over."

"Why am I finding that hard to believe?"

His penthouse apartment had a wall of glass and a view of the Washington Monument. The furnishings were contemporary, tasteful and masculine with the sort of feminine touches an expensive decorator might select. The place could have been featured in a magazine layout, but there was nothing of Reece in the sterile room.

"You can't put her down in here," Kelly protested as he set a squirming Pellonia on the thick geometric throw rug.

"Hey, she already drew blood," he complained, sucking at a scratch on his hand. "It was put her down or drop her."

"But that looks like Italian leather."

"So they tell me."

"Do you know what her claws will do to that?"

"It's furniture, Kelly. Let her explore."

"She needs a litter box."

"I'll run downstairs. Lucy Frangelli has cats. I'm sure she'll let me borrow some food and litter."

"Lucy Frangelli, the mezzo-soprano?"

"Yes, you know her?"

"No, Reece. I know *of* her."

He kissed her forehead. "I'll introduce you later. Wait here. I'll be right back."

He didn't give her a chance to argue and Kelly gazed around the room, feeling more ill at ease by the minute.

"What am I doing here, cat? I'm a builder, not a socialite." She walked to the patio door and looked out. Even his balcony was tastefully furnished.

There was a sudden thump and yowl from the back of the apartment. Pellonia came streaking down the hall toward her.

"Oh, no. What did you break?"

REECE PRESSED THE DOWN BUTTON and waited impatiently. But, when the doors opened, Heath Brockmorton stepped out.

"Reece! Brilliant. We need a chat."

"Later." He tried to push past Heath, but the other man surprised him. Eyes flashing, Heath shoved him back against the far wall.

"Now. We'll go to my flat while you call your Mr. Smith. He will confirm with my Mr. Rigerson that we're on the same bloody side."

As long as Reece had known Heath, he'd never seen this side of his friend before. Heath released him and stepped back.

"Explain Kelvin Tisler."

Heath rolled his eyes. "There is no explanation for that stupid git. I'd no idea they sent him in to do a search. The bloody idiot has a fondness for knives and limited common sense. Pity you only broke his arm. I understand he was shipped home today."

A cold knot formed in Reece's belly. "Oliver Kendall claimed to be dropping Tisler off at the airport as a favor to you this afternoon."

Heath's gaze tightened. "You saw them together?"

"No." He swore softly. "Kendall was watching him check in. Tisler never even looked at him. I even commented on it at the time." He grimaced, disgusted with himself. "Kendall's working for the other side, isn't he?"

"So it would appear. And that would explain where he's getting his funds. Our man on the inside over here was killed."

"Arthur Weems."

Heath raised his eyebrows.

"He was on our watch list," Reece explained.

"Yes. Regrettable, that, but unlike Tisler, Arthur was good at his job."

"He was killed with Gene."

"Yes. We suspect he broke cover to save your friend and the information."

"Did Weems identify the locals involved?"

"All that he could prior to that night. Your people have them under surveillance. I assure you, we're sharing all information at this point."

"You're right. We need to talk."

KELLY HURRIED DOWN THE HALL and stopped as Oliver Kendall stepped out of a bedroom. The gun in his hand had a strangely elongated barrel. Kelly knew she was gaping and forced her lips to close.

"Hello, Kelly. You're looking lovely, as usual. I wish I could say this was a pleasant surprise."

"You're a thief?"

He smiled without humor. "Hardly. You might call me an opportunist. Where is Reece?"

"He stepped out for a moment."

"You're here alone?"

"Except for Pellonia."

His eyes narrowed. "And Pellonia would be…"

"The cat."

"Ah. It gave me a bad start a minute ago. I hope Reece wasn't overly attached to that equestrian figurine."

"What are you doing here?"

He shrugged, taking a step toward her. "Looking for the flash drive, what else? My earlier attempt to get in here and look around was thwarted by an overzealous security guard."

Kelly backed up a step while her heart tried to push its way through her chest wall. He was admitting that he'd killed the security guard? Then he didn't intend for her to live to tell anyone else. She fought an urge to turn and run. The heavy weight of

Reece's gun in her coat pocket brought no solace. She'd be dead before she could reach for it.

Oliver stepped toward her quite deliberately. Automatically, she took another step back. His smile made her shiver. He was enjoying this and that made her angry.

"Don't tell me, let me guess. You're a spy, too."

"Nothing so fancy. I'm a poor working stiff who's being paid a great deal of money to recover the information Reece stole. And they've given me an incentive beyond money. My name appears on a list of their contacts. I can't afford for the wrong people to have that information."

"You work with terrorists?"

His eyes narrowed. "No, I work for those willing to pay me handsomely. Patriotism is overrated, Kelly. It doesn't put food on the table."

"Or a Ferrari in your driveway?"

This time his smile was genuine, letting her see the easygoing man she had first met. "That, too. I need that flash drive, Kelly. Your father didn't have it and it wasn't in his apartment. I admit I was stumped until Reece started hanging around you. There had to be a reason. Obviously, he expected you to recover the drive."

"No."

"Don't tell me you fell for his line? I would have thought you were smarter than that. Reece is a pro,

Kelly. You're playing way out of your league. His family practically mints their own money." His expression darkened. "I need that drive."

She swallowed at the sudden menace. "I'll tell you what I told Heath." She struggled for a calm she didn't feel. "Everyone assumes Curtis Long gave my dad the same zip drive Reece gave him. But, if no one can find it, either the murderer got it the night he killed my dad or Curtis switched it for a fake."

For just a moment, Oliver looked thoughtful. "Nice try. I admit I hadn't considered that possibility, but if Curtis was playing his own game then your dad would have had a fake one when we surprised him." He shook his head. "He didn't."

"*You* killed my father," she breathed, and continued backing up.

"Actually, it was an unfortunate accident. He went berserk even though there were three of us. Military training, if I'm not mistaken. Anyhow, we were trying to get him under control when Weems broke cover and changed sides on us." He shook his head. "Limey whelp. We never once suspected he was a mole. Not once. Okay, that's far enough. Stop right there."

At his words, she stopped moving. Her gaze darted to the front door.

"You'd never make it," he warned agreeably.

"Guns aren't my weapon of choice, but I do know how to use one. You're going to walk out of here with me and you aren't going to say or do anything to alert security or anyone else."

Fear seemed to have rooted her to the spot, but anger swelled in her chest. "Guns make a lot of noise. I don't think you'd risk the attention shooting me would bring you."

"You'd be surprised what I'm willing to risk, Kelly. And this thing on the end of the barrel is called a silencer."

"Shoot me and you've got nothing."

The openhanded slap was so unexpected it sent her reeling backward. Stumbling over the coffee table, she went down, half sprawled against the leather couch.

"You're only partly right. I'd kill you right now, but Reece's interest makes me think there must be a reason not to. Yet. Get up. Slowly!"

Her hand had automatically gone to her cheek. The rage in his eyes was terrifying because it was mixed with a desperation she sensed in every line of his body. Oliver was scared and coldly determined. He would kill her and feel no remorse.

He stepped back when she lowered her hand to push herself up, but the gun never wavered. All thoughts of heroics faded at the expression in his pale gray eyes. The gun in her pocket was a useless weight, but he obviously didn't suspect she had one.

He reached for her wrist and yanked her the rest of the way to her feet. "Walk out of here all nice and cozy with me or I will shoot any fool who gets in my way. I'm not making idle threats."

"I believe you."

She didn't resist when he pulled her against his side. She could feel the throbbing tension in him.

"What will taking me accomplish?"

"Incentive for Reece to find the drive."

"He doesn't know where it is!"

"Then, he'd better figure it out or he gets you back in a body bag like your dad."

"You attacked me at the embassy party."

"Seemed like a good idea at the time. I'm all for seizing the moment, Kelly. I need that flash drive."

He got the door open and half shoved her into the hall. She saw Reece and Heath just past the elevators, talking. As the door closed, Heath saw her and turned. "Kelly!"

Oliver was going to fire. She threw her weight against him a split second before the gun coughed. It spat a bright yellow orange flame and Heath crumpled to the carpet as blood blossomed on his chest.

Oliver yanked her against him, jamming the gun against her face when Reece started toward them. Kelly's hand went into her pocket.

"Stop!" Oliver commanded.

Reece stopped. "Kelly."

Just her name, but a wealth of feeling in his voice.

"The flash drive, Reece," Oliver commanded.

"I don't have it."

"But you can get it."

Reece gazed at her.

"I thought so," Oliver crowed.

Her fingers sought the gun's safety. She was trembling all over, but Oliver didn't seem to notice. His focus was Reece.

"Let her go, Oliver."

"You know better. Back away from the elevator."

"I can't do that."

"Then, she dies right here."

Kelly found the safety. She thumbed it off.

"We can deal," Reece pleaded.

"Where's the flash drive?"

His gaze dropped to her hand in her pocket. "Give it to him, Kelly."

Oliver's gaze whipped to hers. "You *have* it?"

Kelly squeezed the trigger and twisted away as the gun discharged, blowing a hole through her pocket. Had she hit him? Oliver's gun spat again, but amazingly, his shot went into the wall. She yanked the gun from her pocket.

The flash drive popped into the air. Oliver stared and Reece seized the opportunity to rush him.

Kelly saw the muzzle of Oliver's gun flash once more before Reece kicked it from his hand. The gun fell to the carpet as Reece hit him again. Kelly grabbed the fallen weapon and scrambled out of the way as the two men fought. She had seen carefully choreographed martial arts displays before, but she had never seen two people truly using it to harm one another.

Oliver had the edge. Not only was he younger and more driven by desperation, but Reece was fighting with a stab wound.

But then Reece landed a kick that doubled the younger man. Oliver dropped like a stone. Kelly stared, puzzling over the blood staining his side.

Reece crossed to her, hugged her and took his gun from her hand. "You all right?"

"Yes. Your nose is bleeding." She looked at him, dazed.

He wiped at the blood with the back of his arm. "Watch him while I check Heath. If he moves, shoot him again."

"What do you mean, again?" Horrified, she saw the spreading stain on Oliver's side. As she bent to pick up the red flash drive and stuff it back in her other pocket her body began to shake. She'd shot a man.

Reece leaned over Heath, who hadn't moved, and pulled out his cell phone. Things got crazy after that with the arrival of security, the police, paramedics and finally the man Reece called Mr. Smith.

He led them away from the noise and confusion into Reece's apartment where they sat on the sofa side by side.

"You found the flash drive?" Smith demanded of Reece.

"Kelly did."

"Here, take it," she insisted holding it out. "I never want to see that thing again."

"You needn't worry about that," Smith assured her, taking the drive.

"The police—"

"Will be handled. This is a matter of national security."

"Are Oliver and Heath going to be all right?" Kelly asked.

"I'm sure they will, Ms. O'Donnell. Neither injury appears life threatening."

Reece squeezed her hand. "That's good." Kelly was still reeling from the knowledge that she'd actually shot Oliver.

"Ms. O'Donnell, I'm sorry for the loss of your father. I regret that the world will never know that he died in service to his country. The information on this drive may save a lot of lives."

A short time later, Reece ushered him out. Kelly stood, unable to sit still, any longer.

"So that's it? It's over?"

"Actually, I'm hoping it's just beginning." Reece crossed to stand in front of her.

She held out a hand. "Please, don't. I need some time. Some space to think."

Disappointment flashed in his eyes, but he nodded. "I told you I'd give you time. After all, you're still building me a house, right?"

"I thought that was a cover story."

"No, Kelly. I'm serious about the house. In fact, there could be some urgency involved. The management here is tolerant of animals, but I'm not so sure how they'll feel about gun battles in their halls. But you and I will take things slow. I promise."

Chapter Fourteen

"More flowers? Okay, Kelly, I don't care if it has only been a month, if you don't snap this guy up, I'm going to," Leah warned. "He's rich, he's gorgeous, he drives an honest-to-God Lamborghini and he's crazy about you. I want one, too."

"You have Jimmy," Kelly reminded her.

"Let's trade."

A month of casual dates and most of them filled with talk about his house. He'd told her he'd take things slowly and she was the one who'd asked for some time, but in a snail race, Reece Maddox would lose. It was maddening. After all they'd been through together, why was he holding her off like this? He didn't kiss her like a man who'd changed his mind, but something was wrong.

Kelly glanced at the card still attached to the flowers. "These aren't from Reece, they're from James Prince."

If anything, Leah's eyes grew even larger. "What

did you do for the vampire to earn a bouquet of rare orchids? Do you know what orchids cost? These are incredible!"

"I found the perfect piece of land to build Reece his house. That house will put our company on the map."

Leah pulled out the card to read. "Hey. The two of them use the same florist. Man, that florist must think you are one hot mama with all the deliveries they're making here lately."

Kelly gaped at her friend. "What did you say?"

"I said that florist must think—"

"The same florist! The same lawyer, the same security firm, even the same cologne. How could I have been so blind?"

"What are you talking about?"

"I'm an idiot."

Leah sat back in the visitor's chair. "Haven't I been saying that all along? So marry the guy, already."

"That underhanded, sneaky, conniving son of a—"

Leah blinked in surprise. "Which? Reece or the Midnight Prince?"

"Yes!"

"You're starting to scare me here, Kelly."

She snapped off her computer. "You have to leave now."

Leah blinked in surprise. "I just got here. I

thought we could grab some lunch and maybe go to a movie tonight."

"Not tonight. Tonight I'm going hunting."

"You're going to try and catch him again?"

Kelly stared at the replacement photograph of her father that had appeared on the wall of her office. There had been an unsigned note on her desk telling her that all bugs and cameras had been removed. She'd foolishly assumed the note was from Mr. Smith or one of his minions. She'd even hired Mark Ramsey to come in and check the building to be certain they were all gone.

"That…that… Ooh, I could neuter them all."

"See this face? This is definitely fear here," Leah told her. "You want to try talking English?"

"No." She rose and grabbed her purse. "I need to see Mark Ramsey."

"The security guy? Did you find another bug?"

"A big one!"

SHE STRODE PAST Mark's receptionist, dodged a second man who tried to stop her and thrust open the door to Mark's office without knocking. He looked up from a bank of monitors in surprise.

"Ms. O'Donnell! What…"

"You are lower than slug spit and I want back every dime I paid you, you conniving…conspirator!"

"It's okay, guys," he told the men at her back.

"Think again, Ramsey."

He held up both hands. "I told him to tell you the truth! And I never cashed your check so we're even."

"Nothing like."

"Sure we are. Wait until you see what I billed him."

"You're still monitoring Custom Concepts."

"Only the entrances and the parking lots, I swear."

"I am going to wait for him to show tonight and you are not going to warn him, are we clear?"

"No ozone, whatsoever. You do know the guy's loopy over you, right? And he did promise me an invite to the wedding. He loves you, Kelly."

She eyed him narrowly. "I want your word. No interference."

"He's a big client."

"Your word."

"He lent me the money to start Ramsey Inc. Not to mention being a good friend."

She glared.

"Okay. You have my word as long as I still get to come to the wedding."

"There are no other cameras or bugs inside Custom Concepts?"

"None."

As she turned away, she heard him vowing never to fall in love. Instead of going home, Kelly went shopping. It took longer than she'd expected and made a severe dent in her bank account, but she arranged to have everything delivered before 8:00 p.m. Her last stop was the dry cleaners where she'd taken the blue dress to be cleaned.

THE DAY HAD BEEN at least a week long, Reece decided as he parked in back of Custom Concepts. Kelly hadn't answered or returned a single one of his calls today and he had no idea what he'd done to tick her off.

Okay, he'd been deliberately keeping her at arm's length for the past month while he tried to figure out a way to tell her that he was James Prince. He knew he couldn't keep saying nothing indefinitely, but he hadn't come up with a single plan that didn't leave him quaking in fear of losing her for good. He was pretty sure he couldn't wait until their first grandchild was born to tell her the truth. Kelly was smart. Sooner or later, she'd figure it out. He was betting on sooner. A lot sooner.

Reece reached out to unlock the back door of Custom Concepts, remembering how many times he'd nearly blurted out the words when she was talking about James Prince. Each time, he'd stopped himself. She blamed Prince for her father's death. And Gene's death *was* his fault. Reece could barely live with the guilt.

Stepping inside the office, he turned on the light and froze in disbelief.

Paintings graced the walls. An expensive looking area rug with a simple, colorful geometric design covered much of the concrete floor. Along the far wall a leather couch and matching chairs were grouped around a coffee table that held an arrangement of blood red roses and a bottle of wine that poked out of an ice bucket. A pair of wineglasses sat beside an open book on vampires.

He blinked at that item as his pulse began racing. The simple desk had been replaced by an elegant cherry one and instead of the usual sprawl of papers on his desk, a stake and a mallet had center stage. Over the desk hung a mirror.

"If your reflection doesn't show, I'm prepared," Kelly told him.

She stood in the opening across from him, looking fantastic in the silky blue dress with a large silver cross around her neck. Red-gold hair shimmered like a halo about her head and shoulders. His heart beat a rapid tattoo against his rib cage.

"There wasn't time to shift the painters over to do the walls, but I think the dark red would have been overkill, anyhow. I was going to go with a coffin, but that seemed too morbid."

"What is all this?"

"You tell me. You're better at games than I am.

Either you really are a vampire or you're a wealthy investor who doesn't like publicity."

"Kelly—"

"If it's the latter, then this is your office and it should look like an office, not a temporary after-thought you have to sneak in and out of. I'm tired of playing an angel to your Charlie."

"I'm going to fire Mark."

"No, you aren't. He wants an invitation to the wedding."

Reece froze, unable to look away from her, unable to think of a thing to say.

She crossed to the coffee table. "Wine?"

"I love you, Kelly. I think I've been half in love with you since the first time I saw your picture. You were sixteen at the time. Your hair was in a ponytail and there was a smudge of dirt on your face. Your team had just won a ball game thanks to your pitching skills."

Her lips parted. He dared a step forward.

"Your dad was one of the best friends I've ever had. He talked about you all the time. He was so proud. We'd sit around his trailer and talk for hours and he always had new pictures to show me."

Tears welled in her eyes. "I don't understand."

"He found me in an alley getting my butt kicked ten years ago. I would have been killed if he hadn't stepped in and lent a hand. We not only got the information I'd been sent to retrieve, we became fast friends."

"You helped him start Custom Concepts."

"It was his dream," he agreed. He swallowed hard. "It's my fault he died, Kelly. I needed someone no one would suspect to meet Curtis at the airport. I knew your dad would get the drive to Smith, but I didn't know the information was so explosive that the man I took it from would do anything to get it back."

He shook his head. "I was devastated. Losing him…" He swallowed hard. "I let you run the business because it was your right and you wanted it so badly. But I was worried. That's why I kept control. And in a selfish way, staying close to you meant not losing him completely. But I had to protect you."

"Why didn't you tell me?"

He closed the distance between them. "I didn't know how.

"Three words. I'm James Prince."

He dropped his hand to his side, longing to touch her, but afraid she'd step back. "I was terrified you'd shut me out completely once you knew."

"I might have. At first, anyhow. I was furious when I realized the truth this morning. I think I scared Leah. And I know I made Mark nervous."

"Good." They shared a wobbly smile.

"I've had all afternoon and all evening to think things through."

His heart continued racing. "And?"

"Leah reminded me that you own a Lamborghini."

"You're going to marry me for my car?"

She shrugged. "I haven't said yes yet."

Yet. He began to breathe.

"You need a bigger car. The vet says Pellonia's pregnant."

Reece laughed out loud, releasing the incredible tension that had imprisoned him. She smiled, and he knew it was going to be all right. "Come here."

She came into his arms. "By the way, did I mention that couch opens into a bed?" she whispered against his mouth. "With satin sheets?"

"I love you, Kelly O'Donnell."

* * * * *

"Before redecorating a room, I always advise my clients to empty it of everything but one chair. Then I suggest they move that chair from place to place, sitting in it, until the placement feels right. Trust your instincts when deciding on furniture placement. Your room should 'feel right.'"
—TipsFromTeddi.com

Gut feelings. You know, that gnawing in the pit of your stomach that warns you that you are about to do the absolute stupidest thing you could do? Something that will ruin life as you know it?

I've got one now, standing at the butcher counter in King Kullen, the grocery store in the same strip mall as L. I. Lanes, the bowling alley cum billiard parlor I'm in the process of redecorating for its "Grand Opening."

I realize being in the wrong supermarket probably doesn't sound exactly dire to you, but you aren't the one buying your father a brisket at a store your mother will somehow know isn't Waldbaum's.

And, then, June Bayer isn't your mother.

The woman behind the counter has agreed to go into the freezer to find a brisket for me, since there aren't any in the case. There are packages of pork tenderloin, piles of spare ribs and rolls of sausage, but no briskets.

Warning Number Two, right? I should be so out of here.

But, no, I'm still in the same spot when she comes back out, brisketless, her face ashen. She opens her mouth as if she is going to scream, but only a gurgle comes out.

And then she pinballs out from behind the counter, knocking bottles of Peter Luger Steak Sauce to the floor on her way, now hitting the tower of cans at the end of the prepared foods aisle and sending them sprawling, now making her way down the aisle, careening from side to side as she goes.

Finally, from a distance, I hear her shout, "He's deeeeaaaad! Joey's deeeeeaaaad."

My first thought is *You should always trust your gut.*

My second thought is that, *now, somehow, my mother will know I was in King Kullen.* For weeks, I will have to hear "What did you expect?" as though whenever you go to King Kullen someone turns up dead. And, if the detective investigating the case turns out to be Detective Drew Scoones… Well, I'll never hear the end of that from her, either.

She still suspects I murdered the guy who was found dead on my doorstep last Halloween just to get Drew back into my life.

Several people head for the butcher's freezer and I position myself to block them. If there's one thing I've learned from finding people dead—and the guy on my doorstep wasn't the first one—it's that the police get very testy when you mess with their murder scenes.

"You can't go in there until the police get here," I say, stationing myself at the end of the butcher's counter and in front of the Employees Only door, acting as if I'm some sort of authority. "You'll contaminate the evidence if it turns out to be murder."

Shouts and chaos. You'd think I'd know better than to throw the word *murder* around. Cell phones are flipping open and tongues are wagging.

I amend my statement quickly. "Which, of course, it probably isn't. Murder, I mean. People die all the time, and it's not always in hospitals or their own beds, or…" I babble when I'm nervous, and the idea of someone dead on the other side of the freezer door makes me very nervous.

So does the idea of seeing Drew Scoones again.

Drew and I have this on-again, off-again sort of thing…that I kind of turned off.

Who knew he'd take it so personally when he tried to get serious and I responded by saying we could talk about *us* tomorrow—and then caught a plane to my parents' condo in Boca the next day? In July. In the middle of a job.

For some crazy reason, he took that to mean that I was avoiding him and the subject of *us*.

That was three months ago. I haven't seen him since.

The manager, who identifies himself and points to his nameplate in case I don't believe him, says he has to go into *his cooler*. "Maybe Joey's not dead," he says. "Maybe he can be saved, and you're letting him die in there. Did you ever think of that?"

In fact, I hadn't. But I had thought that the murderer might try to go back in to make sure his tracks were covered, so I say that I will go in and check.

Which means that the manager and I couple up and go in together while everyone pushes against the doorway to peer in, erasing any chance of finding clean prints on that Employees Only door.

I expect to find carcasses of dead animals hanging from hooks and maybe Joey hanging from one, too. I think it's going to be very creepy and I steel myself, only to find a rather benign series of shelves with large slabs of meat laid out carefully on them, along with boxes and boxes marked simply Chicken.

Nothing scary here, unless you count the body of a middle-aged man with graying hair sprawled faceup on the floor. His eyes are wide-open and unblinking. His shirt is stiff. His pants are stiff. His body is stiff. And his expression, you should forgive the pun—is frozen. Bill-the-manager crosses himself and stands mute while I pronounce the guy dead in a sort of *happy now?* tone.

"We should not be in here," I say, and he nods his head emphatically and helps me push people out of the doorway just in time to hear the police sirens and see the cop cars pull up outside the big store windows.

Bobbie Lyons, my partner in Teddi Bayer Interior Designs—and also my neighbor, my best friend and my private fashion police—and Mark, our carpenter—and my dogsitter, confidant and ego booster—rush in from next door. They beat the cops by a half step and shout out my name. People point in my direction.

After all the publicity that followed the unfortunate incident during which I shot my ex-husband, Rio Gallo, and then the subsequent murder of my first client—which I solved, I might add—it seems like the whole world, or at least, all of Long Island, knows who I am.

Mark asks if I'm all right. Did I remember to mention that the man is drop-dead-gorgeous-but-a-decade-too-young-for-me-yet-too-old-for-my-daughter-thank-god? I don't get a chance to answer him because the police are quickly closing in on the store manager and me.

"The woman—" I begin telling the police. Then I have to pause for the manager to fill in her name, which he does: *Fran.*

I continue. "Right. Fran. Fran went into the freezer to get a brisket. A moment later, she came out and screamed that Joey was dead. So I'd say she was the one who discovered the body."

"And you are…" the cop asks me. It comes out a bit like who do I *think* I am, rather than who am I, really?

"An innocent bystander," Bobbie, hair perfect, makeup just right, says, carefully placing her body between the cop and me.

"And she was just leaving," Mark adds. They each take one of my arms.

Fran comes into the inner circle surrounding the cops. In case it isn't obvious from the hairnet and bloodstained white apron with Fran embroidered on it, I explain that she was the butcher who was going for the brisket. Mark and Bobbie take that as a signal that I've done my job and they can now get me out of there. They twist around, with me in the middle, as if we're a Rockettes line, until we are facing away from the butcher counter. They've managed to propel me a few steps toward the exit when disaster—in the form of a Mazda RX7 pulling up at the loading curb—strikes.

Mark's grip on my arm tightens like a vise. "Too late," he says.

Bobbie's expletive is unprintable. "Maybe there's a back door," she suggests, but Mark is right. It's too late.

I've laid my eyes on Detective Scoones. And, while my gut is trying to warn me that my heart shouldn't go there, regions farther south are melting at just the sight of him.

"Walk," Bobbie orders me.

And I try to. Really.

Walk, I tell my feet. *Just put one foot in front of the other.*

I can do this because I know, in my heart of hearts, that if Drew Scoones was still interested in me, he'd have gotten in touch with me after I'd returned from Boca. And he hadn't.

Since he's a detective, Drew doesn't have to wear one of those dark blue Nassau County Police uniforms. Instead, he's got on jeans, a tight-fitting T-shirt and a tweedy sports jacket. If you think that sounds good, you should see him. Chiseled features, cleft chin, brown hair that's naturally a little sandy

in the front, a smile that... Well, that doesn't matter.
He isn't smiling now.

He walks up to me, tucks his sunglasses into his
breast pocket and looks me over from head to toe.

"Well, if it isn't Miss Cut and Run," he says.
"Aren't you supposed to be somewhere in Florida or
something?" He looks at Mark accusingly, as if he
was covering for me when he told Drew I was gone.

"Detective Scoones?" one of the uniforms says.
"The stiff's in the cooler and the woman who
found him is over there." He jerks his head in
Fran's direction.

Drew continues to stare at me.

You know how, when you were young, your
mother always told you to wear clean underwear in
case you were in an accident? And how, a little
farther on, she told you not to go out in hair rollers
because you never knew who you might see—or
who might see you? And how now your best friend
says she wouldn't be caught dead without makeup
and suggests you shouldn't, either?

Okay, today, *finally,* in my overalls and Converse
sneakers, I get it.

I brush my hair out of my eyes. "Well, I'm back,"
I say. As if he hasn't known my exact whereabouts.
The man is a detective, for heaven's sake. "Been
back awhile."

Bobbie has watched the exchange and apparently

decided she's given Drew all the time he deserves. "And we've got work to do, so…" she says, grabbing my arm and giving Drew a little two-fingered wave goodbye.

As I back up a foot or two, the store manager sees his chance and places himself in front of Drew, trying to get his attention. Maybe what makes Drew such a good detective is his ability to focus.

Only what he's focusing on is me.

"Phone broken? Carrier pigeon died?" he asks me, taking in Fran, the manager, the meat counter and that Employees Only door, all without taking his eyes off me.

Mark tries to break the spell. "We've got work to do there, you've got work to do here, Scoones," Mark says to him, gesturing toward next door. "So it's back to the alley for us."

Drew's lip twitches. "You working the alley now?" he says.

"If you'd like to follow me," Bill-the-manager, clearly exasperated, says to Drew—who doesn't respond. It's as if waiting for my answer is all he has to do.

So, fine. "You knew I was back," I say.

The man has known my whereabouts every hour of the day for as long as I've known him. And my mother's not the only one who won't buy that he "just happened" to answer this particular call. In fact, I'm willing to bet my children's lunch money that he's taken every call within ten miles of my home since the day I got back.

And now he's gotten lucky.

"*You* could have called *me*," I say.

"You're the one who said *tomorrow* for our talk and then flew the coop, chickie," he says. "I figured the ball was in your court."

"Detective?" the uniform says. "There's something you ought to see in here."

Drew gives me a look that amounts to *in or out?*

He could be talking about the investigation, or about our relationship.

Bobbie tries to steer me away. Mark's fists are balled. Drew waits me out, knowing I won't be able to resist what might be a murder investigation.

Finally he turns and heads for the cooler.

And, like a puppy dog, I follow.

Bobbie grabs the back of my shirt and pulls me to a halt.

"I'm just going to show him something," I say, yanking away.

"Yeah," Bobbie says, pointedly looking at the buttons on my blouse. The two at breast level have popped. "That's what I'm afraid of."

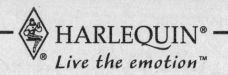

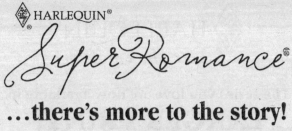

...there's more to the story!

Superromance.
A *big* satisfying read about unforgettable
characters. Each month we offer *six* very different
stories that range from family drama to adventure
and mystery, from highly emotional stories to
romantic comedies—and much more! Stories
about people you'll believe in and care about.
Stories too compelling to put down....

Our authors are among today's *best* romance
writers. You'll find familiar names and talented
newcomers. Many of them are award winners—
and you'll see why!

If you want the biggest and best
in romance fiction, you'll get it
from Superromance!

Exciting, Emotional, Unexpected...

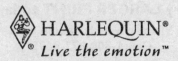

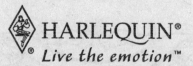

Harlequin® Historical
Historical Romantic Adventure!

*Imagine a time of chivalrous
knights and unconventional ladies,
roguish rakes and impetuous
heiresses; rugged cowboys
and spirited frontierswomen—
these rich and vivid tales will
capture your imagination!*

*Harlequin Historical . . .
they're too good to miss!*

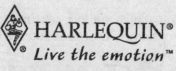